The Man who Shot Jesse Sawyer

When Sheriff Cornelius Doyle is killed, his estranged son Kane sets out to find the culprit, hoping to reconcile with a family that doesn't want to know him – but he soon discovers that his father's apparently honourable life was a lie.

The sheriff had become a legend when he killed the notorious outlaw Jesse Sawyer, but Kane discovers that the facts are at odds with the legend, as Jesse is still alive. With the sheriff's murder apparently being connected to the events of ten years ago, Kane hopes that Jesse can lead him to the killer. Instead he uncovers a dark secret that will not only put his life in peril, but could make it impossible for his family to ever accept him.

The Man who Shot Jesse Sawyer

Scott Connor

A Black Horse Western

ROBERT HALE

© Scott Connor 2018
First published in Great Britain 2018

ISBN 978-0-7198-2696-2

The Crowood Press
The Stable Block
Crowood Lane
Ramsbury
Marlborough
Wiltshire SN8 2HR

www.bhwesterns.com

Robert Hale is an imprint
of The Crowood Press

Typeset by
Derek Doyle & Associates, Shaw Heath
Printed and bound in Great Britain by
CPI Group (UK) Ltd, Croydon, CR0 4YY

CHAPTER 1

'How did you get to hear about this?' Peyton Doyle said when he opened the door.

Kane Bowman met Peyton's cold eyes and spread his hands in an imploring gesture.

'I was in the area when I overheard the news that our father had been shot,' he said. 'I didn't know that he'd died until I got here.'

Peyton sneered. 'My father got shot. Virginia's father got shot. You lost nothing.'

With that, Peyton moved to shut the door but Kane thrust out a hand and stopped it.

'Whatever you think of me, I'm not here to start an argument.'

'Except whatever your intentions, they'll still happen. Now show some respect and stay out of our way. You're not welcome here.'

Peyton shoved the door again and this time, Kane raised his hand, letting it slam in his face. Kane then leaned back against the wall beside the door, looking skyward and taking deep breaths.

The attempt to calm himself down didn't work, but he accepted that the reception he had received was no worse than he had expected, so with a sigh, he trudged away from Virginia's house.

Earlier, he'd learnt that the funeral was to be held later that day so he headed to the cemetery on the outskirts of Union Town. An open hole was situated at the far end of the stretch of land so he stood in front of it for awhile.

He noted that the grave beside the hole was marked as being Ruby Doyle's, and that she'd died less than a year ago. He hadn't been aware of this, but felt nothing other than a vague sense of regret.

After all, Ruby had been the one most adamant that he should be ostracized, and he had no doubt that she had poisoned Peyton's and Virginia's minds against him.

An hour had passed quietly when he sensed movement further into town, so he left the hole and headed to one of the two large oaks that shaded a corner of the cemetery.

The tree was big enough to hide him from casual sight, so he sat back against the bark and wiled away another hour until a line of people came closer. He stood upright in the shadows and watched the procession approach.

A coffin was being carried, with Peyton leading the group. He didn't look Kane's way.

Kane judged that there were so many people here, the entire town had probably turned out to pay their respects, and when the procession came closer, he saw that Virginia was walking behind the coffin. He reckoned that as she turned to enter the cemetery, she glanced his way, but showed no sign of having seen him.

With, presumably, only the family and close friends heading to the graveside, the rest of the mourners mingled by the gate, making the presence of a lone man standing beside the oak less obvious.

Then one man, who had been walking some distance behind the procession, came over to stand beside the other oak, making Kane even more confident that his silent vigil wouldn't attract unwanted attention.

Kane stood sombrely while Peyton said a few words over the grave. When the coffin was lowered, he moved back behind the oak to watch the mourners leave.

He planned to wait until everyone had gone and then head back to the stable where he'd left his horse, before leaving town, but heard approaching footfalls. When he leaned forward to look that way, he found that Virginia was heading towards him.

'I gather you were at my house earlier,' she said, these being the first words she'd spoken to him in five years. 'Thank you for coming.'

'I had to, and I'm sorry for what happened,' he

said. Then he rocked from foot to foot as he wondered whether he should prolong this awkward meeting. 'What did happen?'

Virginia looked over her shoulder at the mourners. With the formalities completed, everyone was chatting while Peyton held court to a group of men, a sight that made her relax and come closer to him.

'As I've heard several times already today, for the last ten years, Sheriff Cornelius Doyle dutifully served Union Town and he never once let anyone down, but it's a dangerous job. Last week this outlaw, Valentine Bordey, rode into town and killed him before fleeing.'

Kane waited for more details, but while making her statement, her voice had broken several times and he judged that she didn't want to explain further.

'If the man who killed Jesse Sawyer couldn't deal with Valentine, I guess that nobody could.'

She snorted a hollow laugh. 'I reckon that only the man who killed Jesse Sawyer could have faced as much danger as my father did.'

'You're saying that his reputation attracted trouble?'

'I am.' She shrugged. 'It also calmed down some situations, but I could tell that he hated being known as the man whose reputation as a great lawman started because he killed that notorious outlaw.'

'That's interesting. I didn't know that about him,

but then again, there's so much I don't know.'

He smiled hopefully, but instead of taking the opportunity to talk more about her father, she backed away a pace.

'Thank you again for coming,' she said, not meeting his eye. She turned away, but then stopped and glanced back at him. 'Take care.'

'I will and if there's anything I can do, just ask.'

She shook her head. 'I just want to be left alone to mourn and look after my family, and Peyton just wants to get back to the task of tracking down Valentine.'

Kane edged forward. 'That sounds like a job that both of Cornelius' sons ought to—'

'No!' she spluttered. 'Peyton's the new sheriff now and don't even think of getting in his way.'

She looked at him with an imploring gaze until he nodded. Then she walked away, back towards the mourners.

Kane watched her go and moved back behind the tree where he did as he had originally intended, and waited for everyone to leave.

Fifteen minutes passed before folks who had been milling around the gate had moved out of view, so he cast a last look at the grave. Then he found that he wasn't the only one who was still here.

The man standing beside the other oak was doing what Kane had been doing, watching the mourners leave, but when he noticed that Kane was looking at him, he came over to join him.

'I had thought you were another one who wasn't welcome here,' he said. 'Then Virginia Wooldridge spoke to you.'

'I'm pleased she did,' Kane said. His mind was to leave now, but the man was smiling benignly making him think that he might learn more about Cornelius' demise from him. 'Does that mean you reckoned nobody would want to see that you were here either?'

'It does, but I had to come, if only to check that he was dead, Kane Bowman.'

Kane looked the man over, confirming that he had never met him before and raised his eyebrows in surprise.

'So, it seems you know who I am, which means you have an advantage over me.'

'There's no reason that you should know me, despite the interest I've had in Cornelius and his family, both the welcome and the unwelcome ones.'

'Who are you?' Kane prompted.

The man licked his lips, his eyes twinkling as he appeared to debate with himself whether he wanted to say more.

'Cornelius Doyle's reputation was built on the fact that he was the man who killed Jesse Sawyer.' The man leaned forward and winked. 'I'm Jesse Sawyer.'

CHAPTER 2

'You look like a man with troubles,' the bartender said.

'It's been a strange day,' Kane said.

He swirled his drink and debated whether he wanted to explain what was on his mind. With a shrug, he ordered another whiskey.

He was in the Red Eye Saloon in Sheridan Pass, five hours' ride from Union Town. The town was nothing more than a gaggle of buildings huddled beside a flag-stop.

Kane had been here only once before when he'd tried to contact Cornelius, and that visit went as badly as his brief meeting with Peyton today. He hadn't intended to come here this time, but Jesse Sawyer had headed this way.

After his revelation at the funeral, Jesse had curtailed their conversation and then walked away, leaving Kane to wonder whether he now knew something momentous about Cornelius or whether he'd been told a joke in bad taste. Either way, he couldn't let the matter end there, so he'd watched Jesse from afar until he'd left town, and then followed him along the rail tracks.

On arriving in Sheridan Pass, Jesse had gone to the town's only hotel, so Kane had headed to the saloon to ponder his next move.

He was sure that Virginia's advice was right, and that Peyton wouldn't welcome him to join in the search for Cornelius' killer, Valentine Bordey. More to the point, he didn't have the necessary skills to be useful.

He found work wherever he could and none of it had ever involved finding someone. Several times he had acquitted himself well in tense situations, but taking on an outlaw who had killed a lawman was a different matter.

In fact, now that he thought about it, he reckoned that even though he had stayed some distance behind his quarry, a man like Jesse had probably been aware that he was being followed, so going after Valentine would be foolish.

Despite that resolution, he still brooded over the matter for several more whiskeys until his thoughts returned to the one mystery that he might be able to solve.

The only thing he'd ever known about his father was that a few weeks after being appointed sheriff, he'd had a showdown with an outlaw who had been responsible for a string of brutal murders. Jesse

Sawyer had bit the dirt, the town had rejoiced, and Cornelius had been revered ever since; except that story might be just that: a story.

He threw a few coins on the bar and with a determined tread, left the saloon and headed to the hotel. He stopped beside the nearest building and looked the hotel over while wondering how he could locate Jesse's room without raising undue alarm.

He decided that his first move would be to get a room for himself, and moved on, but when he reached the corner of the building he heard the sound of grit moving to his side. He started to turn as, in a rush, his quarry emerged from the shadows at the side of the hotel with a gun already aimed at his chest.

'Why are you here?' Jesse demanded.

'After your revelation at the funeral, you can't blame me for wanting to know more,' Kane said, raising his hands.

'I don't, but I told you back in Union Town that you're not getting anything more from me. When I move on in the morning, don't follow me.'

'If you're so determined that I leave you alone, why did you tell me that you're Jesse Sawyer?'

Jesse thought for a moment and then shrugged.

'Because I liked it that someone knew,' Jesse chuckled. 'That secret gnawed away at Cornelius. Now it can gnaw away at you.'

Kane raised his chin. 'It won't be a secret if I tell

people the truth.'

'You can do that, but who would believe you? You're the son of a whore who had a brief dalliance with Cornelius that he never acknowledged.'

'He did acknowledge it. He just never accepted me,' Kane sighed. 'But I guess you're right that nobody would want to believe the truth that you're alive.'

Jesse nodded. 'And that leaves me free to continue being someone who everyone reckons died ten years ago. Anonymity can be useful for a man like me.'

Jesse narrowed his eyes with a warning and took a step away.

'It sounds like you haven't changed in the last ten years. Does that mean you were involved with Valentine Bordey in killing Cornelius?'

Jesse snorted, but didn't reply as he continued to back away. Kane made no aggressive moves, so with a last defiant gesture at him with the gun, Jesse turned away and walked on to the hotel door.

Once Jesse had gone into the hotel, Kane stood for a while, then decided to take heed of Jesse's warning and headed to the stable to collect a blanket. He found a sheltered place between the stable and the station platform, but after his unsatisfactory day, sleep was a long time coming.

He awoke at first light and, contrary to his expectation, he found that the new day had instilled a sense of purpose in him. Despite the fact Sheriff

Peyton Doyle wouldn't welcome his help in finding Valentine, he realized that he didn't care, but needed to search for his own peace of mind, and he knew something that Peyton didn't.

He didn't know whether Jesse's appearance at the funeral indicated a connection to Valentine, but it was a lead that nobody else would follow, so he loitered beside the stable. When Jesse collected his horse and rode out of town, he again followed him, although this time was more cautious than he had been the previous day.

Jesse rode beside the rail tracks at a steady pace and Kane assumed that he would continue along that route until he reached the next town of Martinsville, a journey that should take two days. So, Kane headed south to the base of the higher ground, where he rode on a parallel course to the railroad.

In early afternoon, he reached an area where the railroad was closer to the elevated trail, but Kane headed further uphill to keep his distance from the tracks. When he crested a rise, he was pleased to catch sight of a distant rider.

Kane continued to ride on the higher ground while keeping the rider visible and after two hours, they approached the bridge over Providence Gulch. As the deep gulch and fast-flowing river stretched away for some distance in both directions, Kane had to head back to the tracks. He stopped to watch until Jesse was heading over the bridge, and then moved on.

When he reached lower ground, Jesse was no longer visible, so Kane speeded to a fast trot. The terrain was rugged enough to provide him with adequate cover, so he didn't get a clear sighting of the land on the other side of the gulch until he was fifty yards from the bridge.

Jesse was nowhere to be seen and as the terrain beyond the gulch was predominantly flat, he ought to be in clear sight if he had continued riding at the same steady pace as before. Kane drew his horse to a halt and dismounted, then moved on to the corner stanchion of the bridge where he peered ahead.

To his delight, Jesse had stopped on the other side of the bridge. He was leading his horse behind a large boulder, then scurried around a low-lying rock and disappeared.

Jesse's actions suggested that he was lying in wait for him.

Although Kane had arrived at the bridge in time to discover Jesse's plan, he still groaned in irritation as it seemed that despite his precautions, Jesse had been aware that he was being followed.

Kane dropped to his chest and snaked his way backwards from the bridge until he, too, was behind low-lying cover. Then he moved on and found cover for his horse, after which he returned to his previous position to watch the other side of the bridge.

He settled down to see what Jesse did next.

Two hours passed without developments, by which time the sun was approaching the horizon, leading him to conclude that Jesse would stay by the bridge tonight.

As he didn't want to lie on hard ground all night, Kane moved further away from the bridge to seek out a suitably sheltered place. He chose a circular hollow that had a mound around most of its circumference with the lowest stretch facing towards the tracks and bridge.

He lay on his belly below the lip of the hollow and, as the light level dropped, he kept lookout. When he could no longer see the bridge clearly in the gloom, he turned and shuffled away, but then stopped when he saw movement beyond the far edge of the hollow.

As he had kept a careful watch on the bridge, he felt sure that he hadn't just caught sight of Jesse, but he still crawled towards the mounded edge to peer over the top. He could see nothing beyond the hollow other than the nearby dark terrain.

He narrowed his eyes as he tried to discern anything to make him think something was moving out there, but then Jesse spoke up from behind him.

'I told you not to follow me,' he said. 'Then again, you must be one of those fools who never listen to sense, which means you're just like your father.'

Kane shuffled around to lie with his back resting

17

against the side of the hollow. Jesse was standing where he'd been keeping watch earlier, although unlike their encounter the previous night, he wasn't holding a gun on him.

'You're the fool if you thought I'd comply with your demand,' Kane said.

'I accept my mistake, but you won't acknowledge all the mistakes you make until it's too late.'

'I saw that you were lying in wait for me beside the bridge, so I don't get everything wrong.'

'Except you do.' Jesse gestured behind him and along the side of the gulch. 'You didn't see me crossing the bridge and then sneaking around behind you.'

Kane shrugged. 'It's dark.'

'It is, but that's not your biggest mistake,' Jesse smiled. 'I was lying in wait beside the bridge, but I wasn't waiting for you.'

CHAPTER 3

'Who else is following you?' Kane asked.

'That's not important, other than the fact that this man inadvertently saved your life,' Jesse said. 'He's near the bridge now and shooting you would have alerted him.'

'But why are you—?'

'Be quiet.' Jesse raised a hand and when Kane didn't continue speaking, he nodded in approval. 'Stay out of this, or the next time we meet will be the final time.'

Jesse backed away until he was gone from Kane's sight. Kane waited for a few moments then hurried across the hollow to peer over the lip.

Jesse was running away, bent over double while keeping his head turned towards the rail tracks that headed back towards Sheridan Pass. Then he dived to the ground to lie flat, suggesting that he had seen his quarry.

It wasn't light enough for Kane to see the rail

tracks clearly and when Jesse stopped moving, he struggled to see him. Despite Jesse's warning, he couldn't just let him attack this newcomer, so he dropped down on to his chest and snaked his way out of the hollow towards him.

He had halved the distance to Jesse when his quarry rose to his haunches and at the same time, the dark form of a rider came into view. The newcomer was some distance away so was probably on the other side of the tracks, meaning Jesse would need to get closer to him.

Jesse appeared to reach the same conclusion that he wasn't in the ideal position to launch an ambush, and he fast-crawled towards the tracks. The rider carried on along a straight path to a point beside the bridge, showing no sign that he was aware Jesse was approaching.

Kane considered shouting a warning, but the result of startling the man was hard to predict and could lead to his being fired upon.

Despite his reservations, with Jesse moving faster than he was, Kane stopped being cautious and got to his feet. Then, with his body doubled over, he broke into a run, a move that got Jesse's attention and made him swirl round to face him.

Kane reckoned that he'd tested Jesse's patience to the limit and sure enough, gunmetal flashed in the gloom as Jesse aimed at him. Kane threw himself to the ground to lie on his belly, but long moments passed without the gunshot he feared coming.

He risked raising his head, but the darkness was growing deeper by the moment and he could no longer see Jesse. He could still make out the outline of the rider against the arc of lightness on the horizon.

This man had stopped and was facing his way, suggesting he was now aware that something was wrong. Kane figured that as Jesse knew where he was, he shouldn't stay still, so he got to his knees and crawled towards the rail tracks.

He'd covered only a few paces when a gunshot blasted from close by, sending him once more onto his chest. He lay for a moment, but when the rider hastily dismounted, he figured that this man had been Jesse's target.

'Who's there?' the rider called as he dropped from view behind the rail tracks.

Silence greeted him, but the gun report at least gave Kane a clue that Jesse hadn't moved far from the last place he'd seen him, so he resumed heading towards the tracks, giving that area a wide berth.

He kept looking for Jesse, but failed to see him and after two minutes of crawling, reached the higher section of bank on which the tracks lay. He pressed his body to the ground and snaked up the bank until he could put a hand on the nearest track.

There, he paused to look back along the terrain he had covered, but could see only inky blackness.

The moon had been full for the last three nights, so he would have to wait for at least another hour before he got the benefit of better light.

With Jesse intent on starting a gunfight, he didn't figure he could wait that long, so dragged himself up the last stretch of bank and over the top to lie between the tracks. He faced towards the bridge and moved along cautiously, but a scraping noise nearby made him stop.

The sound suggested that someone was doing what he'd done and was climbing up the bank. It had come from the other side of the tracks, so it was likely that Jesse's quarry had made the noise.

He turned in that direction while wondering how to avoid alarming the man, but then a gunshot rattled, the lead pinging off the metal track a foot to his side, sending up sparks.

'I'm not trouble,' he called. 'I'm trying to help you.'

A snort sounded behind him a moment before a heavy weight slapped down on his back, pinning him to the ground.

'You're not helping nothing,' Jesse said as he pressed down on Kane's shoulders.

'I'm not going to let you ambush this man,' Kane said as he struggled to dislodge Jesse.

'You don't know who he is or what he's done.' Jesse moved closer to speak into his ear. 'He could be the man who shot Sheriff Cornelius Doyle.'

'I doubt that an outlaw like you would be going

after Valentine. . . .'

Kane didn't get to complete his retort as Jesse slapped a hand over his mouth.

'Be quiet,' Jesse muttered.

A moment later, Kane felt Jesse tense up as the scraping noise on the other side of the tracks sounded again. Presumably, Jesse's quarry was moving and this time he was closer.

With Jesse concentrating on looking out for the man, Kane seized what could be his best chance to escape. He jerked an elbow upwards, catching Jesse in the ribs and then followed through by twisting away from his assailant.

His movement made Jesse rock to the side, so Kane redoubled his efforts and with a flailing of his limbs and several bucks, he squirmed out from under him. He half-rolled and fetched up with his back resting against a rail track and his legs draped between the tracks, while Jesse fell the other way to go sprawling against the other track.

Kane couldn't see Jesse clearly, but he saw gun-metal flash as Jesse swung his gun round to aim at him. With only a moment to react, Kane kicked out and the heel of his boot clipped Jesse's gun arm, shoving the gun away.

Jesse grunted in irritation and then rocked backwards, moving himself out of Kane's reach. Kane reacted by going in the other direction.

He scrambled across the rail and hurled himself over the bank. He slid down for a few feet before

skidding to a halt with his head pointing downwards, but figured that he'd moved out of Jesse's
line of fire.

He turned, aiming to get his feet lower than his
head and look up the bank, but he'd yet to complete the manoeuvre when Jesse came bounding
over the rail and hurled himself at him. Jesse
caught him about the shoulders and both men
went rolling further down the slope.

The early evening stars made two revolutions
around Kane before he slammed to a stop at the
base of the slope on his side with Jesse lying beside
him. Kane lunged for Jesse's arm, but the roll
down the slope had disorientated him and he
missed, while Jesse twitched a couple of times and
snarled.

Then Jesse slapped both hands around Kane's
neck while rolling forward to clamber on top of
him. Kane gripped Jesse's wrists and tried to prise
them away, but then he realized that if Jesse was
using both hands, he must have dropped his gun
during the tumble down the slope.

Heartened, he continued using his left hand to
try to free himself from Jesse's clutches while slip-
ping his right hand down to his holster. His fingers
had touched leather when Jesse grunted, having
worked out what he was doing.

Jesse retaliated by jerking his hand down and grab-
bing Kane's elbow, halting Kane's attempt to take
hold of his gun. He tugged and for several moments

the two men struggled, Kane endeavouring to escape the constriction around his neck and Jesse trying to move Kane's hand away from his gun.

With every moment that the impasse continued, Kane felt his chest tighten more and motes of light infringed on his vision. Then, with Kane weakening, Jesse forced Kane's arm up, the motion being so sudden that his grip on the neck loosened, letting Kane hurl his hand away.

Jesse went sprawling forward, giving Kane enough space to drag himself free. He rolled, feeling Jesse claw at his back, trying to stop him.

He rolled again and then swung around to face his assailant. At the base of the bank, the darkness was so deep he couldn't see him. He shook himself while taking deep breaths and then reached for his gun.

This time he drew it without problems and aimed into the darkness. He waited, but all was silent.

'You're not so arrogant now, are you?' Kane said, hoping his taunt would make Jesse betray his position.

Long moments passed in silence making Kane accept that Jesse had the patience to wait him out. He started to make his way up the bank, figuring that a height advantage on Jesse would give him the best chance of seeing him.

He had taken three steps when Jesse muttered something from nearby. As Jesse moved quickly, he made a scraping sound, suggesting that he was seeking to confuse him.

A moment later, a dark shape loomed up in front of him. The figure had an arm raised, the outline of a brandished gun visible against the night sky beyond.

The gun was pointed a few feet to Kane's side, showing that his opponent wasn't sure of his position, but Kane must have made a noise as the gun twitched towards him. Fearing that his assailant would shoot him the moment he worked out his exact location, Kane turned his gun on the figure and fired.

A groan followed by a thud could be heard as the figure dropped from view and rolled down the bank. Kane hunkered down to stay out of sight and trained his gun on the spot where the body had come to rest.

Another low moan and a rattling wheeze sounded. Then silence returned.

'You're safe now,' Kane called. 'I've shot him and I reckon he's dead.'

'I reckon you're right,' a voice said with a light tone, the sound coming from further along the bank.

Kane whirled round, but couldn't see the speaker. With a wince, he realized that the voice had been Jesse's, his jocular delivery different to his usual terse manner of speaking.

'Jesse?' he murmured.

'It is, and you sure are your father's son. Just like

him, you shot the wrong man!'

Jesse laughed. Then footfalls sounded as he moved away into the night.

CHAPTER 4

The morning found Kane in poor spirits.

The previous night, he had confirmed that the man he'd shot, was dead. Then he had dragged the body away from the bank and back into the hollow.

He had spent the night lying propped up facing the dead man. Jesse hadn't returned, but even if he had, Kane was so morose he probably wouldn't have defended himself.

He had never hurt anyone badly before, never mind kill them. Admittedly he had been prepared to kill Jesse, but was only trying to help the dead man before his unexpected arrival had forced him to defend himself.

The sun was high enough to shine down into the hollow when Kane examined the body. His first clear sighting of the dead man's face made him frown as a twinge of recognition hit him.

He thought back and recalled seeing this man at the funeral. One of the mourners by the gate, Kane had noticed him because he had glanced at him, although now he presumed that the man had been looking at Jesse, standing behind him.

With a small mystery solved, he knelt by the body and went through its pockets. He found nothing that would identify him, and when he rounded up the man's horse and investigated his saddlebag, the only item of interest was a scrawled note from someone called Noah Tennant requesting a consignment of lumber for his ranch in Green Valley.

Kane didn't know whether this man was, in fact, Noah Tennant, but as Green Valley was the next town along the tracks after Martinsville, it was probably the man's destination. With that information all he was likely to find out now, Kane hoisted the body on to the back of the deceased man's horse.

He mounted up and led the horse to the tracks and across the bridge. He stopped to confirm that Jesse had moved on before he resumed his journey alongside the tracks.

An hour had passed when he flinched, realizing that he had set off for Green Valley without thinking. It hadn't occurred to him to leave the body and flee, and his willingness to face the consequences helped to alleviate some of his guilt.

With that thought, he rode tall in the saddle. He had never been to Green Valley before, but figured it would be at least another day's ride beyond Martinsville, so he maintained a steady, mile-eating pace.

Through the morning, he still looked out for

Jesse, but saw no sign of him or anyone else. The only incident to relieve the monotony came when a train passed by, going in the opposite direction.

In the afternoon, he approached Martinsville, but not wanting to open himself up to questions about the body, he gave the town a wide detour before moving back to the tracks.

That night he settled beside another bridge where he lay the body down on the ground. Unlike the previous night, he ate from his supplies and as he was likely to reach his destination tomorrow, considered what he should say when he got there.

No matter how he looked at it or what the result might be, the only option that felt right was to tell the truth and let others decide whether his actions could be excused.

The next day he set off before first light and was rewarded when, in early afternoon and sooner than expected, he espied a town ahead, presumably Green Valley. This time he didn't try to avoid anyone and a few miles out of town, came across a wagon that was heading across the tracks.

He hailed the driver who stopped and eyed the body on the back of the horse, with concern.

'I'm looking for Noah Tennant's ranch,' Kane said.

The man didn't look away from the body as he gestured over his shoulder and then moved on without uttering a word. Kane took this as confirmation that the dead man wasn't Noah, as the man would surely have reacted differently if a local rancher had died.

A few miles further on, he approached a sprawling ranch house set within a perimeter fence in the process of being constructed. The two men erecting the barrier stopped working and came over.

Even before they reached him, one man slapped a hand to his forehead and the other man paused and shook his head before moving on.

'I said that Finnegan would come back to us,' one man said when they reached the horse. 'Then again, I never thought he'd be strung over the back of a horse.'

'With Finnegan, I guess it was always going to come to that,' the other man said.

Kane dismounted and introduced himself, learning that the two men were Zackary Michigan and his brother, Driscoll. Zackary hurried away, calling out for Noah to come, leaving Driscoll looking at Kane in the obvious hope that he'd explain what had happened.

Kane only wanted to tell his story once, so waited until Zackary returned with several ranch hands. One of these men stepped forward and leaned down to check the face before he turned to Kane.

'Finnegan O'Neil worked for me until he left without explanation last week,' he said, his statement identifying him as being Noah. 'It's not unexpected that he's returned like this.'

With Noah supporting Driscoll's opinion, the

Michigan brothers exchanged glances while the other men murmured to each other, also affirming Noah's comment. Kane cleared his throat.

'I'm sorry to tell you this, but I shot him,' he said.

His declaration silenced the group while several men edged towards him. Noah raised a hand, making them stop.

'Explain,' he said.

'It happened two days ago beside the bridge over Providence Gulch. It was an hour after sundown and in the dark, Finnegan startled me, so I—'

'You don't need to go on,' Noah said with a sorry shake of the head. 'If you hadn't have killed him, he'd have probably robbed you.'

Kane lowered his head and took a deep breath. He had rehearsed what he wanted to say, and he'd intended to provide a full explanation of the incident. While not identifying Jesse Sawyer by name, instead he started at the end and tried to excuse his actions.

'I don't reckon that was his intention.'

Noah looked him over and then nodded.

'I can see that you're troubled by this, but the fact that you've travelled for two days to return his body, tells me everything I need to know about the incident. Come inside and tell me the whole story. Then I'll report what happened to Sheriff McKinney. I'm sure he'll see it the same way as I do.'

Kane took Noah's offer and headed to the ranch

house while Noah dallied, ordering the ranch hands to deal with the horses and the body. When Noah joined him inside, he took him to a kitchen and poured them both a coffee, after which Kane started his tale from the beginning.

He explained how an unknown man had attacked Finnegan and how he'd tried to help out, but in the dark, Finnegan had been on the receiving end of a bullet. Kane reckoned that his explanation made his actions sound inept, but Noah had set his jaw firm with a look that said he'd already made up his mind.

'It does sound as if this man wanted to harm Finnegan,' he said when Kane had finished. 'I'm sure he had a good reason.'

Kane sipped his coffee and sighed. 'I'm getting the feeling that you don't want me to blame myself about this.'

'I don't. Finnegan came to work for me six months ago and nobody will miss his sour temper.'

'Your workers looked more annoyed than you do.'

'They are, but their sort will support each other no matter what.' Noah sipped the rest of his coffee and put down his mug before standing up. 'I'll go to see the sheriff now. Wait here until I get back and feel free to find something to eat.'

Kane fingered his mug as he forced himself to dismiss the matter in the way that Noah had. With it now looking as if he wouldn't face repercussions, his thoughts returned to his original reason for following Jesse.

'While you're gone, do you mind if I talk to your workers about Finnegan?' Kane shrugged when Noah looked surprised by his request. 'I'd like to find out as much as I can about him and I'd welcome the chance to tell them what happened to him, too.'

Noah still shook his head. 'The Michigan brothers are the only ones who spent much time with Finnegan and I don't want them distracted. Since Finnegan left, that fence has been taking too much time to build.'

Kane thought for a moment, and then smiled.

'In that case, perhaps you'd welcome a suggestion.'

Five minutes later, Kane was standing with Zackary and Driscoll while Noah explained to them that as they now had a replacement worker to help, if they wanted to continue working here, they would meet his deadline of finishing the fence in a week. Kane was relieved that the brothers nodded in approval, although when Noah left to head into town, Zackary eyed him with concern.

'So, do you plan to kill us two next?' he asked when Kane got to work digging the next hole.

'There's no need for comments like that,' Driscoll said, but Kane directed a benign smile at both of them.

'I didn't take no offence,' he said. 'You two worked with Finnegan and you have the right to be wary of me, but part of the reason why I took this job was to put your minds at rest about what happened.'

'And what's your other reason?' Zackary asked.

'I need the work.'

Both men snorted with laughter and with Zackary smiling, it looked as if he might be prepared to give a fair hearing. While they worked, he told them the story he'd told Noah. When he'd finished, Driscoll sighed.

'Finnegan was a whole heap of trouble,' he said. 'One day his ways were sure to catch up with him, so it doesn't surprise me that sneaking around in the dark was what got him in the end.'

Driscoll looked at Zackary, who mustered a half-hearted shrug before offering his own opinion.

'I guess it doesn't surprise me either,' he said. 'I just wish it hadn't have happened. Finnegan did get into trouble, but he knew how to enjoy himself, too.'

'Usually it was at other people's expense.' Driscoll smiled, but when Zackary scowled he spread his hands. 'But I guess not always.'

With Zackary grunting that he agreed, the three men then devoted themselves to working diligently until Noah returned. As the rancher was alone, Kane continued digging until Noah drew up beside him.

'Sheriff McKinney doesn't need to talk to you,' he said. 'He accepted what I told him, and he'll report the incident to the new sheriff in Union Town. So, you can get back to work and not worry about a man who wouldn't have given the matter a second thought if he'd have accidentally killed you.'

Despite Noah's worrying mention of Peyton Doyle, Kane thanked him and resumed work. When Noah headed back to the ranch house, he noted that Zackary cast an aggrieved scowl at Noah's back and then at him.

'If it helps, I won't be taking Noah's advice,' Kane said. 'Killing a man doesn't sit well with me.'

Zackary gave a slow nod, suggesting this declaration had helped him. They worked until sundown without discussing the matter again, the number of posts planted showing that they would have to work hard every day if they were to meet Noah's deadline.

That evening they ate with the other ranch hands outside the bunkhouse. Kane was pleased that nobody looked at him oddly, suggesting that Noah had spoken to them about Finnegan's demise.

As darkness fell, the hands headed into town in small groups in search of entertainment, but the brothers showed no inclination to join them.

'We usually stay here at night,' Zackary said, his downcast gaze and Driscoll's snort hinting that there was a reason he didn't want to mention. 'You can go with the others.'

'I haven't had regular work for a while, so I'll save my money,' Kane said.

The brothers murmured that they agreed with this plan. Then the three men started a fire, using the offcut wood they'd collected during the day and sat around it, enjoying the flames.

They passed an hour in idle chatter until, without Kane's prompting, the conversation drifted back to Finnegan.

'If Finnegan was here, he'd now tell us another tale about his exploits,' Zackary said.

'I can't take Finnegan's place as I haven't had many exploits,' Kane said, 'but I'd welcome hearing about one of his adventures.'

Zackary rubbed his jaw as he appeared to choose one, but Driscoll shook his head.

'He probably made most of them up,' he said. 'Even Finnegan couldn't have got into as many scrapes as he claimed he had.'

'His tales couldn't have all been lies,' Zackary said. 'He always got nervous when someone new arrived at the ranch.'

'You reckon he was worried that someone would come looking for him?' Kane said when Driscoll nodded.

'I reckon so, and when he left, we both thought it was because this man had found him.'

Kane leaned forward in anticipation of learning something useful.

'Did he ever say who was after him?'

'He did.' Zackary raised an eyebrow. 'He said it was a ghost.'

CHAPTER 5

'I assume the man who was after Finnegan wasn't an actual ghost,' Kane said.

'I assume so,' Zackary said with a smile. 'Finnegan reckoned this ghost was armed and vengeful, but he didn't want to talk about who it was.'

'Except he told you enough for you to reckon he'd left to try to avoid him?'

Zackary and Driscoll glanced at each other and shrugged before Driscoll replied.

'We reckon he left to meet someone,' he said. 'He often mentioned Valentine Bordey, who also feared that this ghost would seek him out.'

Kane firmed his jaw to avoid reacting to this revelation and waited to hear more details, but the conversation then turned to other matters, suggesting that these men didn't know anything more. Kane didn't risk making them suspicious of his motives by trying to steer the conversation back to Finnegan, as he was content to have learnt several significant facts.

Clearly the ghost was Jesse Sawyer, a man who everyone assumed was dead except for, presumably, Cornelius, Finnegan and Valentine. In addition, the opportunity to meet Valentine was likely to be the reason why Finnegan had gone to Union Town.

Kane didn't know how he could use this information to find Cornelius' killer, but he stopped dwelling on the matter when the brothers' chatter petered out and they looked at the bunkhouse.

Kane turned to find that five men were trooping around the side of the building. They were all carrying cudgels.

'So, you two haven't come into town for the seventh day in a row,' one man said, setting himself before the brothers with the other four men flanking him.

'We're saving our money, Riley,' Zackary said.

'That's wise, but you're running out of time to pay back what you owe me and staying here won't earn you enough.' Riley laughed. 'You need to come into town and try your luck at the poker table again.'

'That's what got us into this trouble in the first place. So we'll stay here and work hard. When we've finished our latest task, we'll see you again.'

Riley licked his lips and glanced to either side at the other men, giving them a silent order that made them raise their weapons.

'I've been talking to your fellow workers. They

don't reckon you'll earn enough from finishing the fence to even pay off the interest you owe, never mind the whole debt.' He took a long step forward, the other men matching his movement. 'So, we've come to give you a hint of what'll happen if you don't find another way to pay me back.'

The brothers shuffled backwards seeking to put the fire between themselves and their opponents, but Kane reckoned he'd heard enough and stood up to face the leader.

'You've got no right to come here and make threats,' he said.

Riley turned to look Kane up and down. Like the brothers, Kane was unarmed and he sneered at him.

'Stay out of this or you'll struggle to work tomorrow with two broken legs.'

Then he advanced on Zackary, the nearest man, and that encouraged the rest of his men to spread out as they sought to ensure that their targets couldn't flee. Kane reckoned that taking the attack to these men was the best option, so he stepped up to Riley, making him turn away from Zackary.

His exasperation apparent, Riley shook his head that Kane had ignored his demand and aimed a blow at him with his cudgel. Kane had anticipated this move and ducked while moving forward, letting the weapon whistle through the air above his bowed back.

Then he rose before Riley and with the extra

momentum from the movement, delivered a fierce uppercut to his opponent's chin that rocked him back on his heels. Riley shook his head and then aimed a second blow at him.

This time Kane couldn't avoid being hit, but with his opponent standing close to him, Riley couldn't swing the cudgel with much speed and it thudded ineffectually against his upper arm. Kane retaliated with a second swinging punch to Riley's jaw that spun him round and bent him double before being shoved by his shoulders, bundling him over to land on one knee.

Kane then leapt on Riley's back and bore down, forcing his opponent to go sprawling on his front. When Riley hit the ground, the cudgel came free, so with a whoop of delight, Kane scooped it up and raised himself with the intention of bringing it down on the back of Riley's head.

He was still swinging the cudgel back when one of the men came to Riley's aid. This man had been moving in on Zackary, but with Zackary already knocked to the ground and Driscoll being attacked by two men, he came charging towards them.

The man gripped his cudgel two-handed, and on the run, aimed a brutal blow at Kane's chest that would probably crack his ribs forcing him to take evasive action by jerking aside. He rolled off Riley's back, but didn't move fast enough and received a glancing blow to the side that sent him spinning around.

Kane landed on his back, winded and lying beside Riley, where he looked up at his new opponent, who loomed over him, grinning at his success. Then the man brought his cudgel down, aiming for Kane's head.

With only a moment to react, Kane thrust up his cudgel which connected with the descending weapon while still a foot from his chin. The force of the blow drove his own cudgel downwards, catching his cheek, but deflecting his opponent's weapon to the ground.

The man grunted in irritation and then steadied himself to deliver a second blow; Kane made him pay for taking his time when he kicked out and caught the man's knee, making him groan in pain. A second kick to the same knee made him stumble and fortuitously, he barged into Riley who was just levering himself up from the ground.

The man went sprawling over Riley, knocking him back down on his stomach. Kane laughed as he got to his feet, and with both his opponents floundering, swung his cudgel with intent, smacking Riley behind the ear then crunching a heavy blow down on the back of the other man's head.

Both men flopped down, so Kane looked up to seek out his next target. He was pleased to see that both Zackary and Driscoll had rallied, Zackary having gained his feet to take on his two attackers; Driscoll was tussling with one of his opponents, the other man already down, lying on his back beside him.

Kane went to Zackary's aid. He ran around the fire towards Zackary's nearest opponent while shouting to get his attention, hoping to stop his attack.

The man spun around on his heels and with a cry of alarm, raised his hands high. Kane didn't reckon he looked that threatening, but continued running and shouting.

Then he saw that Zackary's other attacker had also stopped his assault and Zackary himself was turning to look past him. Kane ceased his headlong dash and glanced over his shoulder.

Noah Tennant was approaching with three younger men, presumably his sons from what he'd been told about Noah's family. They were all brandishing rifles.

'Stop this fight or I'll end it for you,' Noah shouted, his demand making Driscoll and his opponent separate.

'We weren't fighting,' Kane called. 'Riley attacked us and we were—'

'I see it didn't take you long to start supporting your fellow workers, but I don't care who started this. I don't allow fighting on my land.'

Noah stopped before the fire and signified that Kane, Zackary and Driscoll should stand to one side of the flames and the rest to the other. Riley and two other men needed help getting to their feet, after which they stood hunched over while rubbing sore spots and groaning.

Kane had a few sore spots of his own, but ignored them as he joined the brothers in glaring defiantly across the flames at the men.

'We'll go, but this isn't over,' Riley said. 'Next time you'll get what you deserve.'

Nobody responded to the threat, so with a surly stare at everyone, Riley turned away. His men joined him, heading around the bunkhouse with several of them hobbling. This made Kane and his colleagues smile, although their smiles died when Noah turned to them.

'Consider this your final warning,' he said. 'One more incident and I'll get someone else to finish the fence.'

Noah raised an eyebrow, inviting them to offer an excuse for their behaviour, but as Kane's explanation had been cut off earlier, wisely nobody replied. So, with a last warning gesture with his rifle, Noah beckoned for his sons to join him in heading back to the ranch house.

When they'd moved out of view, the three men turned to each other.

'We sure saw off Riley Payne,' Driscoll said.

'We did, with Kane's help,' Zackary said. 'We're both obliged for that, especially as that wasn't your battle.'

'If it was your battle, it was mine too,' Kane said.

Zackary smiled. 'That's the reason why we supported Finnegan no matter what trouble he got into, or got us into. He always supported his friends.'

'Are you saying Riley came here to hand out a beating because of something Finnegan did?'

Zackary sighed and then beckoned for Kane and Driscoll to join him again sitting in front of the fire. He warmed his hands and rubbed his ribs and shoulder before replying.

'Finnegan won some money at the poker table in Riley's saloon and he got us all fired up with his tales of big bets and the wild times afterwards. We tried to do what he did, but we didn't have his skill and before long, we owed Riley plenty.'

'How much?'

'We need to raise fifty dollars by next week, which is just about the amount Noah will pay us.'

Kane shrugged. 'That doesn't sound too bad.'

'It is. Fifty dollars is the interest on what we owe. Then we have to raise the same amount next month.'

Kane gave a sympathetic frown, after which the three men sat in contemplative silence.

'Unless you can pay off the whole debt, your problems will never end,' Kane said after a while.

'I know,' Driscoll said. 'Riley was scared of Finnegan and that probably stopped him from coming here and threatening us, but clearly, tonight he must have heard about his death.'

'Perhaps he did, but if he's minded to return, maybe I should tell him that I'm the man who killed Finnegan.'

That thought made the brothers smile. Then

they returned to enjoying the flames, but Kane noticed that his companions still often cast worried glances towards the town.

CHAPTER 6

Despite the Michigan brothers' concern about Riley's response to his having been bettered, the next few days passed quietly.

With the fight building trust and common purpose between the three men, they rose early and got to work, and stopped only for minimal breaks until they finished up at sundown. They kept track of the length of fence they would have to plant each day to ensure they completed the job in time, and then made sure that every day they did more.

They were so diligent, the other workers often jeered at them for making everyone else look bad and whenever Noah came near, he appraised their work silently before moving on. After his earlier warning, his lack of a reaction was welcome.

By the time the final day for completing the task arrived, they had only a handful of fence posts left to deal with. Although they still worked hard, Kane let his thoughts dwell on what he would do next.

He had taken this job to get information on Finnegan O'Neil and it had led to the useful lead that the man had known Valentine Bordey. He had stayed on in the hope of getting more details, and to earn some much-needed funds, but since then, when the brothers talked about Finnegan, they hadn't revealed anything of use.

He dropped the name Jesse Sawyer into one conversation, but it had gathered no reaction. He also chatted with the other ranch hands, but they knew even less than his colleagues did about Finnegan's past.

As he had no leads on where Valentine would be, or at least none that would give him an advantage over Sheriff Peyton Doyle, his only option was to assume that as Jesse had wanted to kill Finnegan, he would then go after Valentine.

This meant he needed to find Jesse and let him lead the way to Valentine, and he could start his search by heading to Martinsville to see if Jesse had gone there after the shooting at Providence Gulch.

With that decision made, he devoted his energies to completing their task as quickly as possible. Unfortunately, the last few posts had to be hammered into hard ground, so it was approaching sundown by the time they finished, and Kane was so tired he resolved to wait until the next day before leaving.

The three men slumped down to sit around the final post, and that was where Noah found them when he left the ranch house.

'I see you three are hard at work again,' he said with a jovial tone.

'We reckoned we deserved a few minutes sitting down,' Driscoll said.

'You do. Your final warning still stands, but you've worked hard enough to get paid in full and stay on.' Noah winked. 'You'll be pleased to hear that as a reward, I've lined up a nice, gentle job for you three.'

'I'm sure you have,' Driscoll said with a rueful sigh.

'Except it'll be for two men,' Kane said. 'I'm moving on.'

Noah accepted his declaration without comment and then set about paying them, but when he'd left, the brothers considered him with downbeat expressions.

'I'm sorry you're going,' Zackary said. 'When you arrived, I didn't like you or what you'd done to Finnegan, but I misjudged you.'

'In that case, my time here was well-spent.'

'Why are you in such a hurry to leave? You could spend a while more here and Noah is a decent payer.'

'He is and I am tempted.' Kane tipped back his hat while he considered whether to explain further, but figured that this was his last chance to learn more here and no longer had to be guarded, so he smiled. 'The truth is I'm looking for Valentine Bordey.'

Driscoll smiled. 'From the moment you arrived, I reckoned you had something on your mind. What's your interest in him?'

'Valentine shot up Sheriff Cornelius Doyle in Union Town and I intend to be the man who finds him.'

'So, you're a bounty hunter.' Driscoll glanced at Zackary, who murmured his surprise. 'We should have realized from the way you handled Riley that you're used to dealing with trouble, but we didn't know about this shooting, which means you already know more about Valentine than we do.'

'You did tell me one useful thing,' Kane said, deciding not to correct Driscoll about his motive. 'On the night I accidently shot Finnegan, I thought I was defending him from this other man, and that man was probably Finnegan's ghost from the past.'

'I guess that's possible, but I can't recall anything that we haven't already told you about him.'

The brothers stood in awkward silence as they clearly searched for something useful to say, but when nothing came to mind, they reported that it was time to head into town to meet Riley. Kane joined them in case of trouble and on the way, the two men repeated the stories they'd already told him about Finnegan, Valentine and the ghost they both feared, but didn't add anything new.

As it turned out, the meeting took place in Riley's crowded saloon and Riley accepted their money without rancour other than to declare he would see them again next month. Despite this warning, the brothers were in good spirits as they returned to the ranch, but when they reached the open gates, another meeting was in progress ahead and this one was livelier than their encounter with Riley had been.

Noah was gesticulating to a group of newcomers while his ranch hands crowded around. Everyone was talking over each other with much gesturing and headshaking.

The three men left their horses in the stable and headed over to find out what was going on, but one of the hands saw them approaching.

'There they are,' he shouted, stopping the debate and making everyone swing round to face them.

Then the newcomers spread out and set off walking purposefully towards them.

'I enjoyed those few quiet minutes after we'd paid Riley,' Driscoll said, retreating a cautious pace.

Zackary nodded as he joined Driscoll in backing away.

'I did, too, but I've never seen these men before,' he said. 'So, I don't reckon they're involved with Riley.'

They looked at Kane for support, but he ignored them as he was wondering why the group looked familiar. By the time he'd worked out the answer, the brothers had decided that they didn't need an explanation and broke into a run.

The two men split up, Zackary heading for the fence and Driscoll running to the stable, but the attempt to confuse their pursuers failed. Without breaking stride, half the men ran after Zackary and the rest followed Driscoll. This tactic made Kane check that none of the newcomers were interested in him, which drew his attention to the one man who hadn't joined the pursuit.

Sheriff Peyton Doyle was standing beside Noah and was ignoring the commotion his posse was making as he glared at Kane. When Kane returned his gaze, he looked away to watch the hunt and, as it turned out, it came to a quick end.

As Zackary ducked down to slip through the fence, two men leapt on him and knocked him to the ground. Then he was held down until the rest of his pursuers arrived, after which he was dragged to his feet and marched back towards Peyton.

Zackary's capture appeared to dispirit Driscoll and he stomped to a halt before he reached the stable, but still got the same rough treatment that Zackary had received.

As Kane accepted that he was of no interest to Peyton and his posse, he hurried towards the group and had to fight his way through to the front. He stood in a position where Peyton could see him, but the sheriff ignored him as his men placed Zackary and Driscoll before him and pushed them to their knees.

Peyton produced a rolled up Wanted poster

which he opened and raised so that they could see it. Kane couldn't see who it depicted, although it made Zackary sigh and Driscoll furrow his brow in confusion.

'So, you're going to play it that way, are you?' Peyton said.

'We've heard of Valentine Bordey and we know what he did in Union Town,' Zackary declared. 'But we've never met him, and we don't know nothing about him.'

'So, you're denying that you helped him flee from justice?'

'We sure are,' Zackary spluttered, with Driscoll echoing his plea.

Peyton paraded back and forth before the two men, his slow pacing and smug expression suggesting that he was about to reveal a damning piece of evidence against them.

'Valentine headed this way and I reckon he wanted to meet up with an old friend, Finnegan O'Neil, a man you two know very well.'

Both men lowered their heads as they gathered their thoughts, but didn't need to reply when Noah stepped forward.

'I've heard enough,' he said. 'These men knew Finnegan, but so did I and everyone else here.'

'That doesn't change the fact that they worked with him, and I reckon they know plenty about Valentine, too.'

'I don't reckon they do, but release them and let

them answer as witnesses, not suspects.'

Peyton firmed his jaw, looking as if he wouldn't comply, but then with a short gesture, ordered his men to free their prisoners.

'As Noah said, we can't help you,' Driscoll said, when both men had gained their feet. 'We worked with Finnegan until he left without explanation, and it would have been after Valentine killed Sheriff Doyle. He never came back. Even if he had, we'd have worked with him, but only because we had a job to do.'

He looked at Zackary for support who nodded.

'Yeah,' Zackary said. 'We'll work with anyone. We even worked with the man who killed Finnegan.'

Kane tensed, but Peyton didn't react to this statement, presumably because he'd already been told about his involvement. Peyton glanced at his men, receiving several shrugs and headshakes.

'In that case you're free to go, but if you ever see Valentine again, make sure I'm the first to know.'

Both men nodded eagerly. Then, with the confrontation over, the group broke up.

The workers returned to their business while the brothers headed towards Noah, sporting smiles as they prepared to thank him, although he was still glowering.

Kane expected that despite his unwillingness to talk with him, Peyton would now question him about Finnegan's demise, but instead, he ordered his posse to join him in leaving the ranch. Kane watched Peyton until he was sure that he wouldn't acknowledge his presence and then hurried on to intercept him.

When he caught up with him, Peyton still walked on with his gaze set forward, so Kane hurried past him and stood in his way to make him stop.

'As you must know, I killed Finnegan,' Kane said.

Peyton breathed deeply through his nostrils and Kane started to think that he wouldn't respond, but with his men stopping to watch this encounter, he took a step towards Kane.

'I've heard the story from Sheriff McKinney,' he said. 'Now stand aside.'

Kane lowered his voice. 'You want to catch Valentine more than you hate me. Put that hate aside for a few moments and check that I don't know anything useful.'

Peyton lowered his head and sighed before turning to address his men.

'Everyone carry on back to town,' he said. 'I'll join you shortly.'

Then he headed to the fence where he leaned on a crossbeam with a foot raised, looking at the plains. Kane joined him and matched his posture.

'I saw Finnegan at the funeral,' Kane said, his declaration making Peyton glance at him before he returned to looking ahead, presumably because he hadn't been aware of this. 'The next time I saw him he was about to be attacked by this other man who had also been there. I tried to help him, but in the dark, I accidentally killed Finnegan.'

Peyton raised his chin, and when the silence dragged on for a while confirming that Kane wouldn't offer anything more, he turned to leave. Kane stepped into his path.

'You've made your statement,' Peyton said. 'As I expected, it was of no use. Unless there's anything more, this meeting is over.'

'You had two innocent men dragged across the ranch because they once worked with a man who knows Valentine, and yet you're not even going to question me when I was more directly involved.'

'Nope,' Peyton said, and stepped around him.

'I thought you were better than that,' Kane shouted after him. 'I thought you'd put aside your feelings about me and ask about this other man who was after Finnegan, but clearly, you'd sooner fail to catch our father's killer than get my help.'

Kane set his feet wide apart and placed his hands on his hips, figuring that taunt would get a reaction, and sure enough, Peyton stomped to a halt, looked skyward, and came storming back to stand before him. He jabbed a finger against Kane's chest.

'I know what you've been doing,' he muttered. 'Stop it and stay out of this.'

'Stay out of what?'

'You're a bad liar. After the funeral you got involved in a fight that didn't concern you. Then you got a job here because it'd let you work with two men who might know about Valentine, and you've been questioning the people here about what they know. All that means you're trying to catch Valentine.'

'I guess there's no point denying that I am after him.'

'For the bounty?'

'The money will be—'

'I've had enough of dealing with you, so I give in,' Peyton snapped. 'The bounty to bring Valentine back to Union Town is a thousand dollars. I'll pay you that to just go away and never come back.'

Kane opened his mouth to pour derision on the offer and then closed it as the full ramifications of Peyton's statement hit him. He rubbed his brow and then shook his head.

'You want to preserve the reputation of the man who shot Jesse Sawyer and you reckon that my existence could tarnish it. So, you've been trying to drive me away because you reckon that one day I'll demand money in return for my silence.'

Peyton sneered. 'You could do that and so my offer stands.'

'I don't want your money and I never have. I want to find Valentine so he gets justice, like you do.'

'You're nothing like me.'

Kane smiled. 'I'm not, but your recent behaviour explains why you treated the Michigan brothers like suspects. You've run out of leads and so now you've resorted to following me, trying to build on what I've found out.'

'Except you've found out nothing.'

'That's where you're wrong. I reckon that Finnegan and Valentine are connected to Jesse Sawyer.'

Peyton's eyes flickered with surprise before he hardened his expression.

'I gather that you're moving on from here now, so just do that. Leave, forget about Valentine, and never return.'

With that, Peyton turned on his heel and walked away.

'There's no need to thank me for that information,' Kane called after him, but this time the taunt didn't make Peyton stop and he carried on to his horse.

Kane watched until he'd ridden away and then turned to find that Zackary and Driscoll were standing close by, watching him.

'We've just been told that he's Sheriff Cornelius Doyle's son,' Zackary said. 'So, I guess we can excuse his behaviour.'

'Maybe you can,' Kane said.

Zackary shrugged. 'Are you now leaving to go after Valentine Bordey?'

Kane cast a last glance at the receding Peyton and then nodded.

'There's no reason to delay.'

Kane tipped his hat to both men, but they smiled

and moved closer to him.

'In that case, could you use two new partners to help you find him?' Zackary asked.

CHAPTER 7

'Don't you want to carry on working here?' Kane asked.

'We do, but Noah thought otherwise,' Zackary said. 'He said we'd already had a final warning and tonight's events proved we're too much trouble.'

Kane thought for a moment then held out his hand.

'That's harsh, but you're welcome to join me.'

With their faces lit up with relieved smiles, both men shook his hand then stood back.

'We've just been talking about it and we reckon that as we don't know nothing about taking on outlaws, if we find Valentine, we should split the bounty half for you and half for us. That'll be enough to pay off Riley and still leave some left over.'

'That's a mighty tempting offer, but equal shares for the three of us might be better.' Kane winked. 'I don't know nothing about taking on outlaws either.'

'But you're a bounty hunter.'

Kane shook his head. 'You said I was one and as I didn't want you to know my real purpose, I didn't argue with you. The truth is, Sheriff Cornelius Doyle was my father, too.'

Zackary raised his eyebrows and Driscoll tipped back his hat as they showed their surprise.

'So that means Sheriff Peyton Doyle is your. . . .'

'He sure is, and I'll tell you the rest later, but right now I'd like to get this mission started.'

'That's a good idea.' Zackary glanced at the darkening sky. 'Because we reckon we know where Valentine is.'

On that note of intrigue, the brothers headed to the stable. Kane smiled and hurried to join them.

Fifteen minutes later they were riding out of the ranch, with only a few of the ranch hands coming outside to wish them well. Noah didn't join them.

Zackary directed them to head south towards the railroad. By the time they were riding beside the creek that marked the edge of Noah's land, it was as dark as it had been when Kane had fought with Jesse.

When they approached the rail tracks that marked another boundary for Noah's land, they stopped, and Zackary pointed out the dark outline of an abandoned homestead ahead. Then they dismounted to lie down in the scrub, positioned so they could watch the house.

'What makes you think Valentine's there?' Kane asked.

'We worked it out after the sheriff had questioned us,' Driscoll said. 'Then we decided he hadn't treated us well enough for us to go after him and tell him about this place.'

'The workers rest up at this house whenever the weather turns bad,' Zackary said. 'Yesterday I heard one of them say that someone had been sleeping there recently.'

'The sheriff said that Valentine had headed this way,' Kane said. 'So, it could be him, but it doesn't have to be.'

Zackary shrugged. 'It doesn't, but it's a place to start our search.'

With that sentiment they settled down to watch the house, but when several hours had passed without incident, the deepening cold encouraged them to conclude that Valentine wouldn't come here to sleep tonight. They moved on to the house and, as Valentine could already be there, spread out and checked the building before settling down in a room where the roof was intact.

They got some sleep and in the morning, found a rolled-up blanket in another room that confirmed someone had slept here recently. They found nothing that would identify that person, but when they went outside, they found numerous horse tracks heading away from the building.

Most of these prints would have been made by

Noah's workers and sure enough, many of them trailed along beside the creek back towards the ranch, but they found a recent set on the other side of the creek that went in the opposite direction. They followed these tracks until they lost them over hard ground, but despite that, Kane was content as the hoof prints were heading towards Martinsville.

'I had planned to go to Martinsville before you mentioned this lead,' Kane said. 'So, I reckon this confirms that we're already making progress.'

With this thought cheering them, they rode on. Kane made good his promise from the previous day and told them about his unsuccessful attempts to make contact with a family that didn't want to know him.

'To be honest, I can't see why you care,' Zackary said when he'd finished. 'They hate you and clearly nothing will change that.'

Driscoll shot him a narrow-eyed glance after his unsympathetic comment, but Kane nodded.

'I agree, but I still want to do the right thing,' he said. 'At least then I'll have done everything I can.'

'Your sister sounded more reasonable,' Driscoll said. 'Maybe she'll appreciate what you're doing.'

'She might. Perhaps as a mother she understands my own mother's position, even if they're very different people.' Kane sighed. 'As a child, I was looked after by whichever saloon-girl happened to be the most free that night and I didn't find out which one was my actual mother until after she'd died.'

'That must have been strange, but it explains why you'd like to at least have someone you can call kin.'

'No matter what happens, I do have someone. That man was Cornelius Doyle and he's dead, and dealing with dead family members is a lot less complicated than trying to get to know the live ones.'

Kane smiled, and the two men joined in. Then they discussed whether they thought Riley Payne would come after them when he learnt that they'd left town without paying off their debt.

Kane tried to offer assurance that provided they raised enough money to pay off the interest by next month, they should be fine, but the brothers were worried enough to often glance over their shoulders. Neither did the suggestion that they could just keep riding and never return to Green Valley offer any consolation, as the brothers didn't reckon Riley was the kind of man to forget a debt.

Despite their concern, they saw no sign of anyone following them and made good time, so it was late afternoon when they approached Martinsville. They stopped on the outskirts of town and when they faced the numerous buildings, the enormity of their task made them all frown.

They needed to find a man who had evaded Sheriff Doyle and his posse, while having no ideas about his location other than the possibility that he had come this way. Kane didn't welcome the thought of wandering around the town in the hope they might get lucky, so he looked further afield.

'Looking somewhere outside town does feel like the better option,' Zackary said, when he noticed where he was glancing. 'But there must be hundreds of places where he could be.'

'Except we reckon he stayed in an abandoned house near Green Valley,' Kane said. 'So, we could try other abandoned houses here first.'

Zackary shrugged. 'Again, there could be a lot of them.'

'There could, but nobody ever claimed this would be easy,' Driscoll said.

Zackary mustered a weary nod, so they looked for a potential first target and that let Kane's gaze alight on the railroad.

'Valentine probably slept in that house because he wanted to meet up with Finnegan and it was the closest he could get to the ranch, but he might also have picked a spot where he was near to the railroad.'

'That's some mighty fine thinking,' Zackary said, brightening. 'That would have given him a way to escape if his pursuers cornered him, and if he did it in Green Valley, he might do the same here.'

With that plan agreed, they turned around and rode away from town while staying beside the tracks and looking out for abandoned buildings. They rode for an hour without seeing anything worth investigating until they reached the area that Kane had passed by on his journey to Green Valley.

As he couldn't remember seeing any buildings beyond this point, they headed back to Martinsville. When they started to explore the other side of town, they soon came across a likely place.

An abandoned station house was mouldering away beside the tracks with several other equally decaying buildings scattered around nearby. If they had, in fact, uncovered his hideout, to avoid alerting Valentine, they rode past the station house without displaying an undue interest in the place and didn't discuss what they had seen until a few miles on.

They agreed to ignore the station for now and carry on, but reached the spot where last week, Kane had left the tracks for a detour around town, without coming across anything else of interest.

'So, we stake out the station,' Driscoll said, getting affirmative grunts from the other two men, as by now it was approaching sundown.

As they headed back towards town, they rode away from the tracks and headed to higher ground. When they crested a mound that let them see the station, a lone rider was heading away, forcing them to ride back from the crest and go to ground.

Then they edged forward on foot. Thankfully, the rider was still turned away from them, although he was moving slowly while peering at the buildings, suggesting he was concerned about what was ahead of him rather than who was behind him.

They watched him until he reached an outlying building where he dismounted and then crept around the side. The man lay on his belly, dropping him from their view in the scrub, but despite being several hundred yards away, Kane had already seen enough to make a confident identification.

'That's Valentine's ghost from the past,' he said.

'He sure is acting as if he reckons someone is hiding out down there,' Zackary said. 'But what makes you think he's that man?'

'I had a brief altercation with him when he attacked Finnegan in the dark.' He glanced at the other two men, who both nodded. 'I also heard an odd rumour when I was in Union Town and piecing this together, I now wonder whether this man is Jesse Sawyer.'

Both men shrugged, making Kane regret telling a small lie and not just relating the full story of his meeting with Jesse at the funeral.

'I reckon you mentioned him once before, but the name still doesn't mean anything to me.'

'There's no reason for you to have heard about him, as Sheriff Cornelius Doyle killed him ten years ago. The rumour I heard is that he's still alive.'

Zackary shrugged. 'Ghost from the past or not, that man still looks as if he knows what he's doing. We need to be careful.'

They all agreed with that view, so for the next half-hour they kept a cautious watch on the scene.

Their policy was vindicated when Jesse became visible to them around fifty yards from the station house, having covered several hundred yards through the scrub without being seen.

The area near the building was devoid of cover, so Jesse leapt to his feet and sprinted to the side of the house where he stood tall. He appeared to be planning his next move, but that decision was taken away when a man came running out from the building.

'Valentine?' Driscoll asked.

'I've never seen him before, but I assume that's him,' Kane said.

Valentine was brandishing a gun and aimed towards the scrub where Jesse had been only a few moments earlier. Then he broke his stride while looking around as he appeared to register that Jesse had moved.

A moment later, Jesse edged sideways along the edge of the building towards him, but when he came into Valentine's line of sight, Valentine acted quickly and fired, forcing him to press his back to the wall. Valentine then took flight, hurtling into the scrub and heading for the higher ground where Kane and the others were watching.

By the time Jesse ventured out from the wall again, Valentine was out of his firing range, so Jesse gave chase.

'Keep on running,' Driscoll said happily as Valentine reached the base of the hill. 'You're heading straight towards us.'

'He is,' Kane said and then frowned. 'The trouble is, so is Jesse.'

CHAPTER 8

Kane and the brothers settled down on the crest of the hill, but the hope that Valentine would deliver himself to them receded when he started running up the hill. He veered away from them and headed towards a collection of angular boulders around two-hundred yards to their right.

They watched him until they were sure of his destination and then worked their way backwards on their chests. When they'd moved far enough that Valentine and the chasing Jesse wouldn't see them, they got up and with their heads down, ran towards the boulders.

They reached the nearest large boulder quickly, and with Valentine running uphill, he probably hadn't reached the first one further down-slope yet. Still, they ventured forward cautiously and when rounding the boulder, they faced a winding path between the rocks that led down the slope.

They conducted a quick debate and concluded that it was likely that Valentine would make his way up this path. So they hurried down the slope, passing several boulders then rounding a curve in the path that let them see that they had covered half of the distance to open ground.

Two massive boulders with flat tops and straight sides were before them on either side of the narrow path. Valentine was still not yet in view, but they stopped and turned to each other.

A round of quick nods confirmed that they reckoned they had found an ideal place to launch an ambush. Then they split up, with Kane and Driscoll taking cover behind the massive boulder on one side of the path, and Zackary hiding on the other.

They hunched down and waited, but after a few minutes, Zackary started glancing at Kane in an agitated manner. Kane gave a calming gesture, urging him to be patient, but Zackary still edged forward while peering at the path.

He moved forward far enough to see most of the route downhill and then jerked backwards in alarm. They all waited to see if Zackary had been seen, but when several moments had passed quietly, Zackary gestured, conveying that Valentine was close by and that he'd stopped.

Presumably Valentine had done what they had, and found what he hoped would be a good position to lie in wait, although in his case, he would be waiting for Jesse.

Another few minutes passed, after which the three men started rocking from foot to foot as they didn't know how long this impasse would last, and all the time not knowing what was happening further down the path.

The dark-red rays of the low sun were lighting the tops of the large boulders, so they had plenty of time before it became dark. Even so, Kane ran his gaze down from the length of lit-up rock to the ground then leaned towards Driscoll.

'I reckon I can climb up the boulder,' he whispered. 'Then I'll be able to see what's happening.'

Driscoll nodded and Kane moved to a fault line that diagonally tracked up the side of the boulder. He started climbing and as he had a wide enough ledge to walk safely, gained height quickly.

Soon he was thirty feet above Driscoll, although Valentine had yet to come into sight. Then the going became even easier for the final part of the climb as the boulder was no longer sheer.

He clambered up the last few feet and rolled on to the flat top where he lay on his side taking deep breaths and looking around. He had a clear view of the buildings beside the rail tracks and the path that Valentine and Jesse had beaten through the scrub, along with the start of the journey they had made up the hill.

On hands and knees, he crawled towards the front of the boulder, dropping down on to his stomach for the last section. When he peered down, he found he was almost above Valentine, who was on Zackary's side of the path.

Valentine was looking up and down the slope with quick, darting movements of the head that suggested the waiting game was playing on his nerves. Jesse wasn't visible, and he'd had more than enough time to catch up with his quarry.

From Kane's elevated position, he could see that although Valentine would be able to use only one route up to the top of the hill, below him there were numerous gaps between the boulders that Jesse could have used to go to ground.

Then Valentine stopped searching for Jesse and instead, turned around and looked upwards. The boulder in front of him had the same kind of diagonal fault line that Kane had used to ascend and after a moment's consideration, Valentine started climbing.

The ledge on his side was narrower than the one Kane had used, so he was slower than Kane had been, and after two minutes, was still less than halfway to the top. Valentine appeared to acknowledge he was making slow progress when he cast a nervous glance to either side, a move that made him sway when he saw how far off the ground he was. Valentine then pressed himself to the rock before he gingerly resumed climbing. Kane noted that on the last section of Valentine's ascent, the ledge was almost non-existent, so, confident that he had plenty of time, he crawled away from the edge and hurried to the side of the boulder.

When he looked down, Driscoll was already

peering upwards, so with gestures, he conveyed what Valentine was doing. Driscoll passed this information on to Zackary, who looked up the side of the boulder on his side of the path.

Zackary pointed out a way up, but Kane shook his head. He indicated to Driscoll that the moment Valentine reached the top, he'd turn a gun on him from his position, and make him surrender.

He would then have to make Valentine climb down into Zackary's clutches, while looking out for Jesse. The brothers returned nods, so he headed back to the front of the boulder.

While he'd been away, Valentine had made good progress and reached the tricky last section. Kane settled down on one knee with his gun aimed at Valentine's back.

Valentine worked his way up until he could place his raised hands over the top of the boulder. Then he inched up the last portion of rock before drawing himself up and locking his elbows with his upper body folded over the edge.

He looked around the top of the boulder. Then with a loud sigh of relief, he scrambled on to the top.

'Drop your gun and raise those hands, Valentine,' Kane said.

Valentine tensed, but stayed looking forward.

'You sound a lot different these days, Jesse,' he said.

'I'm not Jesse. I'm a bounty hunter and you're

wanted either dead or alive.' Kane left the rest of the threat implied as he figured they'd already made enough noise to alert Jesse if he was close.

Valentine got up on to his haunches and turned to face Kane while rolling his shoulders, clearly weighing up his chances.

'So, bounty hunter, what's your name?'

'You don't need to know that, or the names of the other two men who have you surrounded.'

Valentine's shoulders slumped as the fight appeared to go out of him. Then he moved his hand to his holster and tipped out his gun.

'What now?' he asked as he raised his hands to chest height.

'You're right that Jesse is close by, but we're going to. . . .' Kane broke off when Valentine flinched and then looked past him, as if he'd seen movement behind him.

Kane doubted that Valentine had really seen something, but in case this wasn't an attempt at deception, he took a step backwards and to the side. Then, while keeping an eye on Valentine, he glanced in that direction, but saw only the flat top of the boulder.

'That was Jesse,' Valentine said. 'I'm sure of it.'

'Jesse is a sneaky varmint. If you saw something move, it probably wasn't him.'

Valentine uttered a rueful sigh, but then he glanced at his discarded gun, adding further weight to the possibility that he was trying to distract Kane, so Kane signified that he should kick his gun over the edge of the boulder. Valentine licked his lips while he took a pace towards the weapon, his eyes darting furtively to either side.

Valentine then flinched again while looking past Kane, but that only made Kane firm his gun arm and shake his head. Valentine responded by leaping away from his gun to land on his belly, a gunshot ripping out a moment later.

The shot had come from behind Kane, so he turned quickly, seeing Jesse drop from view beyond the far end of the boulder. Kane set his feet wide apart and trained his gun on that spot, but long moments passed without him reappearing.

Kane glanced over his shoulder at Valentine, who was twisting round to move towards his gun, although he became still when he saw that he'd been noticed.

'What's happening up there?' Driscoll shouted from below.

'Jesse's found us, but I've got him pinned down,' Kane called, turning away from Valentine.

He hoped his taunt would make Jesse act, and sure enough, Jesse leapt up into view, but he was ten feet away from his last position. Jesse blasted a wild shot at Valentine and then ducked down before Kane could even aim at him.

Kane muttered to himself in irritation and then took cautious steps towards Jesse's last position. He glanced to either side, keeping watch on Valentine and the end of the boulder, but after three paces he stopped.

Then, in a sudden decision, he turned on his heel and set off at a run. When Valentine saw what he intended to do, his mouth fell open with an alarmed look that suggested he didn't reckon Kane could leap over the gap between the two boulders.

Kane still ran on. He suffered a moment of indecision when the yawning gap down to the path opened before him, but by then he'd committed himself.

As he reached the end of the rock, Valentine scrambled towards his gun, but Kane could do nothing to stop him. He leapt forward and glimpsed Zackary peering up as he tried to work out what was happening.

Then Kane slammed down on the other boulder, hitting the rock with both feet a yard beyond the edge before stumbling forward.

Valentine was close to his gun and he reached for it, but his outstretched hand was still short of its target when Kane steadied himself. He blasted a shot into the rock in front of Valentine's questing fingers, making him jerk his hand back.

Kane strode on and kicked the gun aside, making it skitter over the edge of the boulder. Then he stood back from Valentine while signifying with his gun that he should head to the side of the boulder.

As Zackary had been willing to climb up and help

him, there must be a clear route down on that side. Kane was unsure where that route started, but Valentine still set off while eyeing him as he continued to look for a chance to fight back.

Kane followed him while watching for Jesse. He felt sure that another appearance was overdue, but he and Valentine got closer to the side of the boulder without reprisals.

Then movement caught his attention, but to his shock, it came from their boulder. Kane jerked his gun towards the flicker, but then breathed a sigh of relief when he saw that Zackary had climbed up, after all, and was peering at him with only his head and shoulders visible over the side of the boulder.

'Where's Jesse?' Zackary asked.

Kane pointed at the other boulder. 'He's over there. Warn Driscoll and then cover Valentine as he heads down.'

Zackary gestured at Driscoll and then levelled his gun on Valentine while signalling that he should follow him. When Valentine did as he'd been ordered without complaint, Kane watched the far end of the other boulder while keeping his gun aimed in that direction.

Jesse stayed down and when Valentine had moved out of his view, Kane hurried on. He found that the sloping ledge he would have to traverse was wider than the one he'd used to climb up, and with Valentine seemingly resigned to his fate, Zackary kept him under control with ease.

Kane moved round so that he could walk backwards down the slope, keeping a look-out for Jesse. He had taken a step down the ledge when Jesse leapt up into view, but had now come around to the side of the other boulder.

He was only a few yards from the point where Kane had been standing when he decided to leap across the gap. With Jesse so close, Kane dropped down to press himself to the boulder. Jesse fired, his shot slicing into the rock a few inches away from Kane's right arm.

Kane gritted his teeth and swung his gun towards Jesse, but when Jesse adjusted his aim, Kane chose discretion over returning fire and pushed backwards and slipped over the side. He dropped from view as Jesse's second shot clattered into the rim of the boulder where his body had been lying only moments earlier.

Kane pressed himself to the rock to ensure he had a secure hold. He glanced down and saw that Zackary and Valentine were making good progress, already half way down to Driscoll, who was holding a gun on Valentine, too.

With his gun thrust out, he readied himself to return fire and then rose up. To his surprise, Jesse had moved again and he was trying to do as Kane had done and leap over the gap between the boulders.

Fortuitously, Kane rose just as Jesse was taking his final step before leaping, so without fear of retaliation, Kane blasted a quick shot at him. The lead ripped into rock behind Jesse, who must have thought it had passed close to him, because he twitched, and his leap was weaker than intended.

Jesse went hurtling across the gap between the boulders. He waved his arms as he rose up and then came down short of his target.

Kane followed him with his gun, but didn't fire as most of Jesse's body moved out of his line of sight until only Jesse's hands were visible clasping hold of the end of the boulder. Then the hands dropped from view.

Kane listened, but didn't hear a thud from Jesse hitting the ground.

He considered getting back up on to the boulder, but in case Jesse was laying a trap, he turned around and headed down the sloping ledge after the other two. Valentine had reached the bottom and Zackary was taking his last steps down.

Then Zackary looked up. Kane waved them on while urging them to be cautious, but they must have already decided on their next actions as they headed away from the path, taking a route between the boulders that would bring them out on open ground.

When Kane reached the bottom, they were already thirty yards ahead, but he still hurried back to the path and looked around the side of the boulder. His first glance was downwards, but Jesse wasn't lying on the ground, so he looked up.

Jesse wasn't near the top of the boulder either.

Kane winced and glanced in all directions. He still failed to see Jesse, so with a shiver, turned around and hurried after the others.

CHAPTER 9

Despite the fact Kane didn't know where Jesse had gone, the group reached their horses without incident. Kane told the brothers what had happened on top of the boulder.

They agreed that getting away quickly was their best option. Then they all looked at Valentine.

'I won't give you no trouble,' he said, raising his hands and now appearing docile.

'Your choices are being shot by Jesse or being taken in by us,' Driscoll said. 'Cross us though, and you'll find we're just as much trouble as Jesse is.'

Valentine didn't retort, so they mounted up. Zackary and Valentine rode doubled-up and in the lead so the other two men could watch their prisoner.

Valentine reported that his horse was in the station house, so when they reached the outlying buildings, Kane drew back to take hold of Jesse's horse while the others rode on to the railroad.

When he caught up with them, Valentine had already mounted up, so with a last glance at the scene of the encounter with Jesse, they galloped along beside the tracks.

They had covered several miles before they stopped and took stock of the situation. In their haste to get away from Jesse, they had fled back towards Martinsville, so now turned north and embarked on a circuitous route away from the rail tracks that would take them to Union Town.

After thirty minutes, they released Jesse's horse, and when the level of light dropped, they made camp on high ground where they could see anyone approaching from any direction. Then they tied up Valentine.

Again, Valentine didn't resist, holding out his hands for them to be bound and then sitting down in the centre of the group beside the fire. Only then did Kane, Zackary and Driscoll look at each other and smile as they reflected on the enormity of what they had accomplished.

'Another successful bounty hunting mission completed,' Kane said with a wink to Zackary and Driscoll as Valentine had his back to him.

'We still have to get him to Union Town to collect the bounty,' Zackary said, seemingly not getting the hint that they should appear confident in front of their prisoner.

'We do, but we can handle Valentine and we've left Jesse behind.'

'Jesse won't give up, and he'll know where we're going.'

Kane nodded and used a stick to draw a map in the dirt. He traced out a potential route that would take them to the north of Sheridan Pass. This journey would take longer than the more direct route along the rail tracks, but it would avoid the usual trails, so should be safer.

'We should be fine for the next two days,' Kane said when the brothers had agreed to his plan. 'But you're right and the final leg of the journey could be the most dangerous.'

With that thought they reverted to silence. Later, they divided up the guard duties through the night before settling down.

As it turned out, the night passed without incident and, despite Zackary's concern, the next day they rode towards their first destination without seeing any sign of anyone following them.

Even better, Valentine gave them no trouble. He rode with his head lowered in the middle of the group, and whenever they stopped for a break, he carried out their orders without prevarication.

Late in the day they forded the river to the north of Providence Gulch. Kane feared that Valentine would take advantage of the situation and try to escape, but he did as he'd been told.

That night, Kane still watched Valentine, as he couldn't shake off the feeling that he was only being co-operative to lure them into a false sense of security. He also looked out for the expected retaliatory assault by Jesse, but when the situation hadn't changed by morning, they moved on. With time to think, he tried to foster an opinion about Valentine.

This man had killed his father, but Sheriff Cornelius Doyle was a man he hadn't known, or wanted to know him. So, he felt only a vague sense of satisfaction at having completed a duty he'd set himself, along with an emptiness as he wondered what he would do after collecting the bounty.

The day passed as quietly as the previous one had, and the group only became talkative when they had skirted around the north of the pass that gave the town of Sheridan Pass its name. They had made good time, so if they rode into the night, they would reach Union Town around midnight.

Still fearing that the last leg of the journey might be dangerous, they decided to spend another night outdoors. At sundown, they stopped in a sheltered spot a mile away from the entrance to the pass and started to make camp, but had yet to settle down when, for the first time since they'd captured their prisoner, Kane saw people.

A line of riders was trailing out from the pass. The brothers joined Kane in watching what could be innocent activity, and although they were too far away to identify the group, that possibility diminished when the riders swung round, and at a steady pace headed towards them.

'I assume Jesse works alone, but others could still want Valentine,' Zackary said.

'Whatever the answer, I don't reckon we should wait to get it,' Kane said. He pointed back along the way they had come. 'We've passed numerous places to hole up. I suggest we head back to one of them.'

Zackary and Driscoll nodded and set off for their horses. By the time they'd mounted up, it was clear they hadn't been mistaken, as the riders were heading directly towards them, so they set off at a gallop.

With the brothers leading, Valentine in the middle, and Kane bringing up the rear, they skirted along the base of higher ground. A ridge was to their side along with many gullies where they could hide, provided they could get far enough ahead of the other riders to sneak into one of them without being seen.

To this end, Kane looked back. The riders were still following, but were maintaining their leisurely pace, giving him hope that they had misunderstood the situation.

A mile ahead, an outcrop of stark rock jutted out into the plains. Kane called ahead and drew the brothers' attention to the fact that they were putting some distance between them and their followers and that they should seek cover beyond the outcrop.

Accordingly, they maintained their fast pace until they approached the rocks where Driscoll put on a burst of speed so that he could locate a potential hiding-place. Kane took a last look at the riders before rounding the outcrop, noting they were now some distance behind, but he had to draw back on the reins as Driscoll had stopped after covering only another fifty yards.

The group bunched up as they struggled to control their horses, and when Kane saw why Driscoll had stopped, he snarled in irritation. Another group of riders was approaching from the other direction.

'Our followers didn't speed up because they knew we were trapped,' Zackary said unhappily. He looked around. 'Should we head into the plains or make a stand here?'

'We can't fight off both groups,' Kane said. 'Then again, after a long day of travelling, I doubt we can outrun them either.'

Kane looked at Valentine. Zackary followed his gaze and also considered the third option of handing their prisoner over to these men. Driscoll, however, didn't agree with them and instead pointed at the approaching line of six riders.

'That's Riley Payne in the middle,' he said.

Kane narrowed his eyes as he peered at the riders. When he confirmed Driscoll's observation, he tipped back his hat in surprise.

'In that case, I was wrong,' he said. 'I didn't expect him to follow us this far.'

Driscoll nodded. 'After we captured Valentine

I'd stopped worrying about him, but I guess Riley has a reputation to maintain.'

Kane pointed at the outcrop. 'We'll hole up and try to talk our way out of this. If that fails, we've bettered him once before, so we can do it again.'

The brothers cast sceptical looks at him, but still headed to the outcrop. They all dismounted and while Kane kept watch on Valentine, Zackary and Driscoll sought out cover.

When they'd scrambled into hiding behind a low-lying group of boulders that had tumbled down from the outcrop, Kane escorted Valentine behind cover with them. He sat their prisoner down between him and Zackary and then peered over the boulder before him at the riders, who, as they approached the outcrop, slowed down and spread out.

'Running away was a bad idea,' Riley called when they had come to a halt.

'Following us was an even worse one,' Zackary shouted back.

Kane directed a calming down gesture at Zackary to remind him that they planned to talk their way out of this predicament. Driscoll took up the suggestion by standing up, putting himself in full view.

'We will pay back what we owe you,' he shouted. 'You gave us a month and we intend to use that time to raise the money.'

'Men who plan to pay me back don't sneak out of town at night.'

Riley raised a hand and in a co-ordinated move, his men drew their guns, forcing Driscoll to drop to the ground and the others to duck down. A volley of lead then clattered into the boulders.

'He sure isn't going to listen to reason,' Zackary said.

'And not all of his men are here yet,' Kane said.

Zackary nodded. 'The others will be here in a matter of minutes, which means we have to fight back before they arrive and we become hopelessly outnumbered.'

Kane couldn't argue with that assessment of their situation, so he waited until the shooting petered out and then raised his head, but a second volley ripped out, forcing him back down. The brothers tried to follow Kane's lead, but again were forced to dive for cover as bullets pinged into the boulders and the outcrop behind them.

Zackary tried just raising his gun and firing blind. Surprisingly, a few moments later the shooting abruptly ended.

Kane glanced over the boulder to see that Riley and his men were dismounting, Zackary's retaliation perhaps having spooked them into being more defensive. Kane hurried them on their way with a couple of quick shots before he crawled along the ground to the outlying boulder where he peered around the side.

Riley and his men were no longer in clear view, having taken advantage of the available cover in the undulating terrain. That observation made Kane turn and look up at the outcrop.

A ledge was before him, just above head height. He smiled and then got the brothers' attention.

'Distract Riley with talk about our plans to take in Valentine for the bounty,' he said. 'I'll get to a higher position where I can shoot down at them.'

'That might just lead to him taking our prisoner in himself,' Driscoll said.

Kane shrugged. 'That could be the best option, but it might not come to that.'

Kane shuffled along to the outcrop and got up on his haunches as he picked out the handholds he'd have to use to reach the ledge.

'Riley, we need to talk,' Driscoll called. 'We've caught the outlaw, Valentine Bordey, and once we've claimed the bounty on him, we'll pay you back everything we owe.'

'You varmints couldn't catch a cold,' Riley shouted.

His response encouraged Kane to raise his head. He couldn't work out the exact spot where Riley must be hiding, but as the bar-owner was keeping down, he wouldn't notice when Kane started climbing.

Kane put a foot and hand to the outcrop and then raised himself.

'You don't have to believe us. Just help us escort our prisoner to Union Town and by midnight you'll have your money.'

For long moments Riley didn't reply, giving Kane enough time to clamber up three handholds so that he was high enough to press his belly against the side of the ledge.

'You're lying!' Riley shouted. 'You're trying to distract us.'

Kane assumed that Riley had seen him climbing. Sure enough, gunfire ripped out and peppered the rock to his side, forcing him to redouble his efforts to climb quickly.

He forced himself up the next two handholds and then leapt forward, sprawling on the ledge where he rolled twice in his desperation to get out of Riley's line of sight. Lead continued to whistle through the air, but as none of it hit the rock near him, Kane shuffled around on his chest to face the plains.

He couldn't see Riley's group, but drew his gun as he edged forward. Kane looked for his first target, but groaned before he found one, as the other group of riders came galloping into view around the end of the outcrop, having taken a curving detour to come at them from the plains.

Kane reckoned he had to act before they arrived. He fast crawled forward until he could see several of Riley's men who were looking at the riders.

Kane noticed that the newcomers had drawn their guns and, strangely, were aiming them at Riley's men. He rubbed his brow as the feeling hit him that he had misunderstood the situation, after all.

Then he saw the leader of the new group and couldn't help but smile. Sheriff Peyton Doyle and his posse had arrived.

CHAPTER 10

While Peyton's posse was still a hundred yards away, Riley and his men beat a hasty retreat to their horses.

Kane moved to the end of the ledge so that he could look down at Zackary and Driscoll who were still cowering behind their cover.

'We got it wrong,' he called to them. 'We're being rescued by Sheriff Peyton Doyle.'

The brothers exchanged worried glances, their previous encounter with Peyton still clearly on their minds. Then with a shrug they appeared to accept that he was the lesser of the evils facing them.

They whooped with delight and raised their heads to check out the scene for themselves. Then they started shooting at the fleeing men.

They fired high, but Riley's men still mounted up as quickly as they could. The men cast a last concerned look at the advancing posse, confirming they must have had dealings with Peyton before and set off back the way they'd come.

Riley dallied to shake a defiant fist at the Michigan brothers.

'This isn't over,' he shouted. 'The law can't protect you for ever.'

Zackary fired off a shot, making Riley jerk his shoulders downwards suggesting it had been close, and that this time Zackary hadn't aimed over his head. Riley swung his horse around and galloped off after his men.

The posse then arrived. They stopped in front of the boulders where the brothers were hiding and looked at Peyton for instructions, but the sheriff shook his head.

'Let Riley scurry back to Green Valley,' he said. 'We have bigger problems to deal with.'

The men continued to watch Riley until he was several hundred yards away and it became clear that he wouldn't come back. Then they turned to the outcrop to receive cautious murmurs of appreciation from the brothers. They took hasty steps backwards when Peyton saw who he had rescued and registered his annoyance with flared eyes.

'We're obliged that you put our first meeting from your mind and helped us,' Driscoll said.

Peyton looked them over while shaking his head and his scowl deepened when he saw Kane looking down at him from the ledge.

'If I'd have known Valentine's associates were in trouble, I'd have left you,' Peyton said. 'So, this time show your gratitude by helping me to find him.'

'The last time we met we didn't keep nothing from you, but this time we have something to show you that you're sure to welcome.'

Peyton sneered and folded his arms, defying Driscoll to make good his promise. That sneer faded away when Zackary bent down and rose again holding Valentine by the elbow.

'That's Valentine,' he murmured.

Driscoll smiled. 'It sure is, and we three caught him.'

'How did the likes of you. . . ?' Peyton dismissed the matter with a shake of the head and barked out instructions for his men to take control of the prisoner.

Zackary kept hold of Valentine until the men joined him and then passed him over without comment. While Peyton's men checked Valentine's bonds, Kane clambered down from the ledge.

The brothers cast concerned looks at him, showing that they still weren't confident about how the sheriff would deal with them, so Kane headed over to Peyton to clarify the situation.

'We found him lurking by an abandoned station a few miles out of Martinsville,' he said.

'What made you look there?' Peyton said, his gaze locked on Valentine.

'We'd decided to check out buildings near the railroad and we had some luck.'

Peyton snorted. 'Getting lucky was the only way you'd find him.'

'You're probably right, but all that matters is that Valentine is now in your custody.'

'That's all that matters to me. All that matters to you is getting your hands on the bounty on his head.'

Peyton had put a considerable amount of contempt into his comment, but Kane found that his half-brother's antipathy no longer concerned him now that he'd done what he'd set out to do in delivering Valentine to the law.

'As that's what you think my motivation was, I'd be obliged if you'd confirm that we've done enough to get that bounty.'

'When I get back to town, I'll get the money together as quickly as I can,' Peyton snarled. 'While you wait to collect your blood money, stay out of my way.'

Kane figured that his having to return to Union Town for the bounty was fuelling Peyton's latest outburst of anger, but he ignored it and headed back to his colleagues to give them a thumbs-up signal.

As it was getting dark, Peyton declared that they would camp here tonight. He stationed men at the end of the outcrop and closer to the ridge to keep lookout for Riley and other trouble while ensuring that two men stood guard over Valentine at all times.

Peyton didn't speak to his prisoner. He also

ignored Kane and the brothers, as did the rest of the posse, so the three men ended up sitting together with the outcrop at their backs, watching the camp-fire and relaxing.

When Peyton's posse set about feeding themselves, they ate their own rations, after which everyone became more animated.

Later, two men came over to ask them for more details about how they'd captured Valentine, an action that made Peyton cast aggrieved glares at them.

Kane took the opportunity to annoy Peyton more by spinning out a lengthy tale about Valentine's capture. He didn't hide Jesse's involvement, although he avoided mentioning him by name, a revelation that would have been sure to initiate an argument with Peyton.

The tale gathered the attention of others in the posse who came closer to hear it, leading to Kane having to restart his story. Soon, everyone other than Peyton and the men guarding Valentine had gravitated towards Kane and they all nodded and muttered in approval whenever he described a crucial part of the incident.

Such was everyone's delight that when he had finished, Kane half-expected that he would be asked to tell the tale again. That didn't happen, but as the men spread out around the fire, their murmured comments along with their bemused glances at Peyton showed that they were wondering why their successful hunt hadn't gathered the sheriff's approval.

Kane noted that Valentine also looked at them oddly. He presumed that Valentine had noticed his avoidance of mentioning Jesse and so when it came time for the guard and lookout duties to change, he volunteered to guard Valentine next.

Peyton stood up and started to make what would probably be a refusal, but Kane's offer gathered support from his men and so with a shake of the head he sat back down again.

The brothers then volunteered to help with the next lookout duty, which garnered no opposition, so once they'd headed into the darkness, Kane found himself sitting in front of the prisoner while another man stood behind him.

Valentine cast several significant glances at him suggesting he wanted to speak his mind, but an hour of the two-hour duty passed without him talking. Only when someone by the camp-fire started singing, initiating a round of rowdy comments for the singer to be quiet, did he lean towards Kane.

'Your story sure got everyone's interest,' he said.

'Including yours it would seem,' Kane said levelly.

Valentine licked his lips and then lowered his voice, even though the other guard was still close enough to hear him.

'I was interested in the part of the story you

didn't tell.'

'If I'd related everything, the tale would have taken all night and I'm sure Peyton wouldn't have accepted me doing that.'

Valentine chuckled, as if their guarded conversation had confirmed his suspicions.

'I'm sure he wouldn't, and I sure won't be the one to fill in the rest of the details. I know when it benefits me to be silent, too.'

Kane nodded. 'That's the right thing to do. Nobody wants to hear what you have to say, not now, not ever.'

'Except now, with all these witnesses, might be the only time I can speak. Once I get to Union Town, I don't reckon I'll live for long enough to have my say in court.'

Valentine then looked at Peyton, indicating who he thought would silence him. Despite his low opinion of Peyton, Kane shook his head.

'The sheriff will let justice take its course.'

Valentine snorted. 'The former sheriff used to say things like that, but I know the truth about him. That's why I had no choice but to kill him while I still could.'

Kane opened his mouth to continue trading words with the prisoner, but decided that it only ran the risk that Valentine would talk about Jesse Sawyer, so he caught the other guard's eye. They changed positions, making Valentine scowl, but he reverted to silence and for the rest of Kane's guard duty, said nothing else.

When it came time for him to be replaced, the rest of the men were trying to get to sleep, so with nobody paying him any attention, Kane headed over to Peyton.

'You've not spoken to your prisoner,' he said.

'He'll get to speak his mind in court,' Peyton said. 'Even then, I don't need to be there to hear it.'

'Perhaps you should make sure that he knows it's in his best interests to keep quiet. While I was guarding him, he hinted that he knows a secret. So perhaps he wants to bargain with you about whatever he—'

'I'm not taking your advice and I don't care what he has to say. He's not talking himself out of having his neck stretched.'

Peyton set his hands on his hips and glared at Kane, but Kane didn't respond, figuring that he'd done his best to warn Peyton. Now it was up to Valentine how he dealt with the information he had.

With Zackary and Driscoll heading back towards the camp, he turned away to join them, but with a snort of exasperation, Peyton then headed towards the prisoner. Kane ignored him until he met up with the brothers and they'd resumed their earlier position at the base of the outcrop.

Peyton stopped in front of the prisoner, who got up on his haunches and said something quietly for Peyton's ears only. Peyton shook his head and glanced around.

Only the guards and Kane's group were watching them as the rest of the men were either asleep or sitting down after completing their duties. Valentine followed Peyton's gaze and appeared to note the lack of interest in him with a wide smirk.

Then, without warning, Valentine leapt towards the nearest guard. He slammed into his lower chest, head first and carried the man backwards for several paces until they both tumbled over.

The other guard and Peyton hurried towards them as Valentine rolled away from his opponent and then rose up. Surprisingly, he was no longer bound and had wrested a gun from the supine guard.

Before Valentine could raise the gun, Peyton drew his own and fired at him from only a few feet away, the crack of the shot sounding louder than usual in the night.

Valentine uttered a groan of pain and then stumbled. His gun fell from his grasp before he toppled over to lie on his front.

As everyone around the camp leapt to their feet and hurried over to help deal with the situation, Peyton walked forward to stand beside Valentine.

He kicked him over and shook his head at the sight of his unmoving body. Then he walked away.

CHAPTER 11

'Did everyone see what just happened?' Peyton said when he faced his posse.

'Nobody's going to say that you didn't have just cause to shoot that varmint,' one man called.

'That's not what I asked. Did everyone see that Valentine slipped his bonds, got hold of a gun and was planning to shoot his way to freedom, giving me no choice but to kill him?'

'That's exactly what I saw,' the same man replied.

His comment started a round of similar comments, even though most of the men had been asleep or hadn't witnessed the incident. Peyton appeared to acknowledge that he knew this when he headed over to Kane.

'And you?' he asked.

'I saw the whole thing,' Kane said. 'Valentine said something to you and you turned away. Then Valentine took advantage of the fact that few people were watching him, to mount an escape attempt. Somehow he'd removed the bonds from his hands and he. . . .'

Peyton opened his mouth wide with a mime of a yawn.

'You sure do like to spin out a yarn,' he said, raising a laugh from his men. 'An acknowledgement that my report was accurate will do.'

'It was, although I don't know what he said to you.'

Peyton shrugged. 'It wasn't important. He just said that he knew.'

'Then I guess that now we'll never know what that was.'

Peyton didn't react other than to turn away to order one of his men to throw a blanket over Valentine's body and for the men who weren't on lookout duty to go to sleep.

The men did as he'd requested and settled down with little chatter, but the shooting ensured that another hour passed before anyone slept. Kane still had too much on his mind to join them.

'So, Peyton shot up Valentine,' Driscoll said after a while. 'I can't help but feel he put aside his duties as a lawman and acted in revenge.'

'So do I,' Kane said. 'He could have tried to subdue the prisoner and ensure that he got him back to town to face justice in court, but he gunned him down instead.'

The two men looked at each other and frowned, but Zackary shook an admonishing finger at them.

'If he did use the situation to kill him, I wouldn't blame him, but you're being too cynical. We all saw what happened. Valentine got hold of the guard's gun and then tried to escape.'

Kane opened his mouth to respond, but then limited himself to a sigh, as having voiced his concern, he accepted that Zackary was probably right, and he was letting his animosity towards Peyton cloud his judgement. With nobody offering any further opinions, they joined the others in trying to get to sleep.

Despite Kane's unease over the matter, his tiredness after the day's exertions meant that he fell asleep quickly. In the morning he still felt on edge, although he couldn't identify the exact reason why. Even so, he didn't talk again with his associates about the previous night's incident and he avoided Peyton.

Valentine's body was slung over the back of a spare horse and they started the journey back to Union Town. Peyton's men were eager to return home after a lengthy time away searching for Valentine, although Peyton was as subdued as Kane.

The group rode at a fast trot to the railroad and then stayed beside the tracks. As a result, it was early in the afternoon when Kane first saw the town ahead.

He beckoned to his colleagues to draw back. He waited until the rest of the riders had moved ahead of them before speaking.

'Peyton said he'll get the bounty money together quickly,' he said. 'I don't know how long that'll take, but hopefully we won't have to stay in town for long.'

'That worried look on your face suggests you don't welcome going there,' Zackary said.

'You're right. I can't shake off the feeling that Peyton used the situation at the outcrop to take his revenge on Valentine, so I don't want to ride into town with him and be a part of his victory parade.'

'The sheriff isn't triumphant about how the search for Valentine ended, but I get your point. You should put some distance between you and Peyton, while Driscoll and me stay close to him and make sure he doesn't forget about our money.'

Zackary glanced at Driscoll, who nodded, so Kane pointed to a saloon on the outskirts of town.

'We'll split up and meet later at the Long Trails Saloon.'

'Hopefully we'll have good news,' Zackary said then frowned. 'Although we'll have to talk about how we deal with Riley.'

'And Jesse, too,' Driscoll added. 'He's another man who probably never forgets about being bettered.'

All three men winced. Then the brothers turned away and trotted after Peyton.

Kane waited until the riders had disappeared

into town. As he doubted he'd ever visit Union Town again, he decided to make a last trip to the cemetery.

He rode around the outskirts of town and when he approached the oak tree where he'd stood during the funeral, he saw that he wouldn't be alone. His half-sister, Virginia, was kneeling beside Cornelius' grave.

Before Peyton had killed Valentine, he had considered seeing her again to see if they could forge a common understanding between them, but now he didn't feel inclined to speak with her. He slowed down as he searched for the best place to go to ensure that she didn't see him, but on the exposed hill, only the two oaks were available.

Then even that possibility disappeared when she stood up and turned towards him. She put a hand to her brow to shield her eyes from the sun, and when she confirmed his identity, she nodded and stepped back to await his arrival.

Now having no choice, he rode on and dismounted at the gate. He walked on to stand in front of the grave where he avoided meeting her eye by looking at the wooden cross that had been erected.

'Your brother has returned to town,' he reported.

She shuffled from foot to foot. 'For you to know that, you must have spent time with him.'

'I did.' He coughed to clear his throat as he accepted that he was using clipped tones and she didn't deserve to be treated harshly. He turned to her and softened his voice. 'You need to know that Valentine Bordey is dead.'

She gasped and lowered her head for a while, then with a deep breath, stood beside him facing the grave.

'I would have preferred him to face justice, as I'm sure Pa would have done, but at least this brings an end to it.' She glanced at him and gave a thin smile. 'And perhaps it might bring a start.'

'Perhaps,' he said, now finding that he felt relieved that they'd met up, after all. 'I doubt I'll ever make a fresh start with Peyton, but I'd like to get to know you better.'

'In that case, there's no need to delay. I'd be delighted if you could come to my house for dinner tonight.'

She had spoken quickly, and rubbed her hands, suggesting the chatter and animated movement was helping her to avoid dwelling on Kane's news, but Kane still shook his head.

'I'm grateful for the offer and I will take it up one day, but I'm not sure tonight is a good idea.'

He smiled in the hope that she wouldn't ask him for more details, but she frowned.

'I know this is a big step, but delaying won't make it any easier. If it helps, Peyton will be busy with clearing up what happened to Valentine and then dealing with anything that's happened while he's been away, so he won't have to know.'

'It's not that. I'm worried that the situation with Valentine isn't over yet. I fear that another man was involved with him and that man might go after me next. I wouldn't want to put you and your. . . .'

She put a hand on his arm, silencing him.

'I'm standing in front of the grave of a man who never shied away from trouble and that man's daughter is no different. You will come to dinner tonight.'

'Yes, ma'am,' Kane said.

She breathed a sigh of relief. 'Despite your differences, you also need to trust that Peyton knows about and deals with any trouble that goes on in his town. He'll stop this man if he tries anything.'

'He already knows that another man connected to Valentine is out there,' Kane said with a smile as he stretched the truth for her benefit. 'So, I'm sure you're right.'

She nodded then beckoned for Kane to join her in leaving. They faced the grave one last time before they walked towards the gate.

'I am right,' she said. 'Our father will always be known as the man who shot Jesse Sawyer, and I'm sure that one day, Peyton will be known for something just as significant.'

'I hope he. . . .' Kane trailed off and came to a halt, as Virginia's mention of Jesse set off a train of thought that led him to a conclusion that he hadn't considered until now and which probably explained Peyton's recent behaviour.

'What's wrong?' Virginia asked.

He set off walking again. 'Nothing, but maybe I do need to speak with Peyton again.'

CHAPTER 12

'I should have known you'd want to get your bounty money quickly,' Peyton said when Kane came into the law office and stood before his desk. 'As I told your friends, it'll take a few days to get it together. They've already started the wait in the Long Trails Saloon.'

Then, with a quick lowering of his head, Peyton returned to reading the report he'd been examining before Kane had interrupted him. Kane stayed where he was so Peyton ignored him.

Kane didn't mind the wait as it gave him time to put his thoughts in order. It didn't make him any less angry.

Two minutes passed and as the report was a short one, Peyton put it aside and then read a second one. This was the only other piece of paper on his desk, so when he'd finished that, he moved to get up, not looking Kane's way. His irritation got the better of him and he flopped back down and faced him.

'You know,' Kane said simply.

'What's that supposed to mean?' Peyton said with a sneer and leaned back in his chair.

'It means what I said. You know.'

Peyton looked him over and then shook his head.

'Leave. I have a patrol to make with my deputies.' Peyton gestured at the two men standing by the door. 'I'm not wasting no more time on you.'

'Your deputies can deal with that routine matter. Then you and I can talk.'

Peyton got up and came around the desk with a hand thrust out ready to grab Kane's arm so that he could, presumably, escort him out of the office, but Kane stood his ground. Peyton stomped to a halt and then with a sigh, gestured at the deputies to leave without him.

'Talk,' he said when they had gone.

'You know the big secret that nobody was supposed to know,' Kane said. 'Except you've never suspected that I know it, too.'

Peyton stabbed an angry finger against Kane's chest.

'Quit with the babbling and just say what's on your mind.'

Kane folded his arms and then glanced around the room making an obvious show of checking that they were alone.

'Sheriff Cornelius Doyle was not the man who shot Jesse Sawyer.'

'What kind of. . . ?' Peyton trailed off and then stepped back to sit on the edge of his desk. 'What do you reckon you know?'

'That Jesse Sawyer didn't die. That Finnegan O'Neil and Valentine Bordey were running from Jesse. That I accidentally did Jesse's work for him when I killed Finnegan. That you deliberately killed Valentine to silence him.'

Peyton snorted. 'In other words, you don't know nothing.'

'You can't dismiss all that as nothing. You executed a prisoner just to keep your father's reputation from being tarnished.'

'I didn't. Your hatred of me is stopping you from believing what you saw with your own eyes. You hadn't secured Valentine's hands properly and after I took custody of him, he seized his last chance to escape. He got hold of a gun and I had to shoot him to protect my men.'

Kane shrugged, unwilling to concede that this version of events was an accurate reflection of what he'd seen.

'I'm sure everyone in your posse will back you up on that, but how can I be sure when you had everything to gain from his death?'

'Because what you reckon you know isn't a big enough secret for me to kill to protect it. My father's reputation came from ten years of dedicated service to this town, not from an event that hardly anyone can remember clearly any more.'

Kane narrowed his eyes. 'That was an odd choice of words, again. You're saying that what I know is unimportant, which suggests there's an even bigger secret connected to Jesse that I don't know about yet.'

Peyton glanced aside before shaking his head.

'I've humoured you for long enough. I should have gone with my instincts and had you run out of town the moment you walked in here.'

'Now I know you're hiding something. The more worried you are the angrier you get.'

Peyton snarled and then with a sudden movement, leapt up from the desk, launching a punch at Kane's face. Kane jerked his head back while thrusting up an arm to defend himself, but Peyton's fist brushed his arm aside and caught him with a scything blow to the cheek.

The force of the punch knocked Kane back for a pace and spun him round. He righted himself and rocked back towards Peyton, aiming to repay him in kind, but walked into a second punch that crunched into his chin and sent him reeling.

He toppled over and when he hit the floor, skidded along for several feet before he came to a halt. While lying on his back he shook himself then raised his head to find Peyton standing over him with a fist drawn back.

'Get up so I can knock you down again,' he muttered.

Kane snorted a harsh laugh. 'Keep getting

angrier so I can work out what you're hiding.'

'I'm not hiding nothing about our father. I'm just protecting this town from no-account varmints like you.'

'You just called Cornelius "our father" and you've never done that before. You sure must be worried, and I'm going to find out why.'

Kane shoved himself backwards across the floor to move away from Peyton and then sat up. Peyton didn't move towards him and still didn't move when Kane stood up.

'Don't,' Peyton said, his voice still raised. 'This doesn't have nothing to do with you.'

'I'm not leaving until you tell me the truth. Jesse is still alive and I reckon he'll try to kill me, and I reckon you're not safe either, and perhaps even Virginia.'

Peyton had been shaking his head, but the mention of his sister made him turn around to face the window.

'How did you find out about him?' he asked, lowering his voice as he appeared to get his anger under control.

'Jesse was at the funeral and he told me who he was.'

Peyton gasped in surprise. 'Why would he talk to you?'

'He claimed that he wanted someone to know. That sounded strange, so I followed him to Providence Gulch.'

'So, Jesse was the man who attacked Finnegan in the dark and he was also the man you had to fight off to capture Valentine?'

'He was, and that's sure to have made him angry. Even if he finds out that you made sure Valentine won't talk, I doubt that'll be the last we hear of him.'

Peyton turned away from the window to face him. He lowered his voice to a menacing growl.

'This is the last time I'll tell you that I didn't kill Valentine to silence him.'

Kane shrugged. 'Maybe you didn't, but it doesn't change the fact that with one bullet, you protected your father's reputation and resolved the mess Jesse was trying to clear up.'

'What do you think that mess was?'

'I don't know what Jesse's motive was. Maybe he wanted to kill the men for something that happened between them years ago, or perhaps he was just trying to eliminate two people who knew he was still alive.'

Peyton shook his head and then gestured at the door.

'You're wrong, but you don't need to know the truth. I'll make sure your bounty money is available tomorrow. Then you and your friends can ride off and find somewhere safe to hole up while I deal with Jesse.'

'No deal. Like your sister said, Cornelius never ran from trouble and so his son sure isn't going to do that.'

Peyton's mouth dropped open in shock. 'You've met her since we came back?'

'I have, and tonight we're having dinner. Then I reckon I'll stay on here and get to know her better while I wait for Jesse to—'

'Enough!' Peyton snapped then stormed across the office to stand before him. He bunched and raised a fist as if to punch him again, but then with a snarled oath, lowered it. 'So, you want to know the truth, do you? You want to hear about the family you're trying to get to know?'

Kane nodded. 'Whatever Jesse's done, I need to know.'

'Jesse's done plenty, but that's not important.' Peyton stepped closer to him. 'The important thing is that Pa let him.'

'I don't know what you mean.'

Peyton pursed his lips, as if he already regretted providing his short explanation. Then he stalked back to the window to look outside, and this time Kane joined him. The two men stood in silence.

'The mess Jesse was clearing up wasn't of his own making,' Peyton said after a while. 'It was Pa's. While he was our sheriff, Pa gave him the names of men he wanted killed and Jesse always got the job done. That's why Union Town has been such a peaceful place. Anyone who was too much trouble, quietly disappeared.'

After that revelation, an even longer silence

reigned until Kane coughed.

'I don't know how to respond,' he said. 'I can't believe that a lawman would ever agree to that sort of arrangement.'

'I don't know the full story, but I reckon it started out as something else. Pa genuinely believed that he'd killed Jesse, but later, Jesse showed up, which meant he must have killed an innocent man. Pa kept his mistake a secret and Jesse took advantage. When Jesse killed other rival outlaws, Pa turned a blind eye to his activities and so an arrangement was born.'

Kane thought for a moment and then nodded.

'So, Finnegan and Valentine were on that list of men who were too much trouble?'

'I can never know for sure, but I assume they were and they worked out that with Jesse on their tails, their days were numbered. As they didn't want to take on Jesse, Valentine decided to kill the easier target.'

Kane frowned. 'Except that plan was unlikely to work because once Jesse has been given a mission to complete, he never gives in.'

Peyton nodded. 'That was his reputation before he *died*, and you were right about one thing: he won't stop killing and we could be his next targets.'

'It's a sorry tale, but I can understand how it could have happened. Last week, when I took the small step of following Jesse, I'd never have believed I'd end up here, so maybe the first step taken by

Cornelius ten years ago felt like it'd be a small one, too.'

'Perhaps, but that's the truth about Sheriff Cornelius Doyle and Jesse Sawyer.' Peyton turned to him. 'So, do you still want to have dinner with my sister tonight?'

CHAPTER 13

'We're going to be here for a while,' Kane said, when he joined the Michigan brothers in the Long Trails Saloon.

'Peyton said it'd only take a few days to get the bounty money together,' Driscoll said. 'And I got the impression that to get rid of you, he'd do it as fast as possible.'

'Since then things have changed. I talked with Peyton and we sorted out plenty, but we also raised a whole heap of problems.' Kane leaned on the bar between them and drew them closer. 'We're sure that Jesse will come for us. So, it'd be safer if we all stayed in town until he's been dealt with.'

Driscoll frowned. 'I don't like the thought of sitting around waiting for someone to come and shoot us up. I reckon we should go after him.'

'Finnegan and Valentine both knew that you don't go after men like Jesse, so we'll stay in the Empire Hotel and watch out for each other. At the first sign of trouble, we'll all take him on.'

Driscoll glanced at Zackary, who nodded.

'I guess we can wait, but if you're that worried, maybe we shouldn't do that waiting in full view of anyone walking into the saloon. We should go to the hotel now and see about getting something to eat.'

'You should do that. I'm dining with my sister tonight.'

Despite the gloomy assessment of their position, the brothers smiled broadly and slapped him on the back. Then, while both men congratulated him on making progress, they headed to the door.

They glanced around town to check that nobody was paying them undue attention and then moved on to the Empire Hotel, but when they got there, to Kane's surprise, Peyton was standing by the door waiting for him. The brothers acknowledged him and headed inside, leaving Peyton to gesture to the stables where Kane had left his horse.

'I reckon I'll join you for that meal,' he reported.

'As I said earlier, the first step is often small and—'

'This hasn't got nothing to do with my accepting you. I just need to make sure that my sister is safe, and to make sure you don't tell her what we discussed. She doesn't need to know what her father did.'

Kane shrugged. 'As I want this evening to be a success, even without that warning, I wouldn't have talked to her about it.'

Peyton bunched a fist. 'See that you don't.'

Kane glanced at the fist and then shook his head.

'For all these years I've thought that I wasn't good enough to be a part of the Doyle family. It turns out that all along I was better than you.'

'I don't care what you think about us as long as you keep quiet.'

'I will, but that doesn't mean I approve of what Cornelius did and I hope that one day the truth about him does come out, but I won't be the one to reveal it.'

Peyton set his jaw firm, but didn't reply, so Kane headed off to collect his horse. When he returned, Peyton was mounted and waiting for him.

Peyton hurried on ahead. With Kane trailing behind, still looking out for Jesse, the two men headed to the small house that stood at the base of a hill around five miles out of town.

Virginia was standing outside, looking anxiously in their direction, presumably fearing that Kane wouldn't come, after all. The sight of Peyton riding ahead of him made her put a hand to her mouth before moving on to the corral gate at the side of the house to welcome them.

'I'm pleased I cooked plenty,' she said lightly when they'd dismounted, although her voice broke, confirming she was trying to cover her nervousness with good cheer.

'After several days of trail rations I'm looking

forward to eating until I burst,' Kane said with a smile.

They both turned to Peyton to continue the good humour, but without comment, he walked by them and into the house. Virginia looked at Kane with raised eyebrows, but Kane didn't think he could provide an adequate explanation of the current situation between them, so went inside.

Peyton was already making a fuss over two small children, so while Virginia dealt with preparing the table for dinner, Kane joined Peyton. As he had little experience of children, he soon felt uncomfortable and gravitated back to the table to join Virginia.

'Their names are Harry and Katherine,' she said.

'You have a charming family,' Kane said. 'Will your husband be joining us?'

'He had to go to Independence City after the funeral,' she said. 'He's due back on the noon train, tomorrow.'

'What does he do?'

She glanced at him quizzically as if he ought to know, and then shrugged.

'He's US Marshal Hank Wooldridge. He was annoyed that this appointment meant he couldn't help Peyton search for Valentine, but he had to give evidence in a trial and he never neglects his duty.'

'I have heard of him, but I hadn't connected him to you.' Kane laughed. 'So, you married a lawman.'

She smiled. 'I reckon that only goes to prove that

a love of justice is in the blood.'

Peyton snorted, making Virginia glance at him, but when he didn't say anything, she went to the cooking pot and peered inside. Dinner was declared ready and, as she reported that the children had eaten earlier, Peyton took them to a back room before joining the others at the table.

She filled three bowls with stew that had plenty of potatoes and green chillies. For the next five minutes both men murmured their approval between mouthfuls while Virginia glanced up appreciatively from her own bowl.

When he'd finished, Kane fingered his bowl wondering if it'd be polite to ask for a second helping, but Virginia provided one without need for a request and then moved to fill up Peyton's bowl, but he shook his head.

'I ate earlier,' he said.

'Then I'm even more pleased you came,' she said with a significant glance at Kane, although that only made Peyton sneer.

'I didn't come to eat your excellent dinner because of him. I'll be stopping here tonight to keep an eye on things.'

'Kane's already told me that you fear Valentine had an associate who might cause trouble, but you should concentrate on finding him and not worry about me. I can take care of myself and my family.'

'I know you can, but I'll still do what I reckon is necessary.'

She sighed, but then nodded and with them saying nothing else, Kane raised his fork.

'As will I,' he said.

'You're not staying here, too,' Peyton said. 'You'll go back to town and wait with your bounty hunter friends for me to end this.'

'I'll do that, but as I said: I'll do what I have to do to deal with any trouble that follows me after Valentine's death.'

Peyton mustered the briefest of nods while Virginia smiled at Kane.

'I didn't know you'd teamed up with bounty hunters,' she said. 'Then again I did say that justice is in the blood.'

Kane nodded. 'I found Valentine, but Peyton's timely intervention made sure that I didn't lose him.'

'In that case, I'm pleased you worked together to deal with him.'

'We didn't work together, and he's not got justice in his blood,' Peyton snapped. 'I arrested Valentine for justice. He found him for the bounty.'

Virginia shook her head. 'Whatever the reason, I'm relieved you found him. As you have to find this other man, you and Kane should do whatever you did with Valentine again and—'

'Do not take his side,' Peyton said, slamming his hand on the table, rattling their bowls. Then, with a shake of the head, he got to his feet and headed to the door. 'I'll be outside keeping watch. I'll come back in when he's gone.'

With that, he stormed outside leaving Virginia and Kane facing each other.

'Perhaps you shouldn't say anything that sounds like you're taking my side,' Kane said.

'I can do that, but I'm surprised you're taking his side.'

She laughed and so Kane lightened the tension by chuckling.

'That was the first time the three of us have eaten together. I'm aware of the strain that puts on him.'

'I have no problem eating with you. After you and Peyton dealt with Valentine, whatever the circumstances, it should have helped him to put aside his anger to deal with this new situation.' She glanced through the window to watch Peyton walk up to a corner post in the corral. 'Except he's even more annoyed with you than before.'

'I reckon that's because we were talking about Valentine,' Kane said, figuring that he ought to provide an explanation to stop her poking away at the problem and perhaps working out Peyton's secret. 'Peyton had to kill Valentine when he tried to escape and, like you, he'd have preferred him to face justice.'

'I didn't know that.' She rubbed her jaw and then smiled. 'So perhaps when things are less fraught, the next time might go better.'

'Perhaps,' Kane said. He stood up. 'As I don't want to cause any more trouble, I'll go back to town while it's still light.'

She nodded, and after thanking her for the meal he headed outside. He had intended to go to his horse and leave, avoiding the risk of provoking another argument, but to his surprise, Peyton beckoned him over to the corner post.

'Jesse's here,' Peyton said when Kane joined him. He pointed at the post where a Wanted poster detailing Valentine's crime had been pinned.

Kane frowned. 'That's clearly a warning, but he took a risk sneaking up to the house to deliver this message.'

'He must have thought it worth doing.'

Peyton glanced at the window, but Virginia wasn't watching them, so he removed the poster and turned it round for Kane to read the writing on the back.

'By noon tomorrow,' he said, reading the message. 'I guess the threat is obvious, but what does he want before tomorrow?'

Peyton stuffed the poster in his pocket, but didn't reply, so Kane looked around for any sign of Jesse. Peyton gestured at him to turn away from the post and face the door.

'Keep your eyes on the house,' he said. 'We weren't inside for long and he can't have gone far. My best guess is he went over the hill behind us.'

'Then we have enough time to run him down.'

'This could be a trap, so I'm not leaving Virginia. You'll go after him.'

Kane smiled. 'Virginia will be pleased that we've joined forces.'

'We haven't. I'm just hoping Jesse will use you for target practice and betray his position.'

Peyton then moved on to the door, so Kane wasted no time in mounting up. By the time he was riding away, Virginia was looking through the window, clutching a rifle.

Kane followed Peyton's hunch and without wasting time looking for tracks, took a direct path up the hill, figuring that this would either lead him to Jesse or give him a good vantage point to survey the surrounding terrain.

As it turned out, Jesse wasn't lurking at the top of the hill, but when Kane stopped and looked back, he confirmed that this was an excellent place to keep watch on the house. He tracked along the crest, noting several mounds that Jesse could have hidden behind, before reaching a steep slope down the side of the hill that led to the plains and away from the town.

This route could have let Jesse get away quickly, so he dallied to look for tracks, finding deep, recent ones in soft earth at the top of the incline. He headed down the hill and when he reached the bottom, accepted that Jesse could have gone in several different directions, so looked for more tracks.

It was still an hour before sundown, so he had plenty of time to track him today, but failed to find any prints. After fifteen minutes of fruitless searching, he had to accept that riding off without clear proof that he was going in the right direction was probably doomed to fail, and he returned to the house.

Peyton came outside to meet him and hear his report.

'I reckon Jesse headed away from town, but I don't know where,' he said, finishing off.

'Go back to town,' Peyton said. 'Then keep your head down until noon tomorrow has come and gone.'

'The same goes for you, but it'd help us to work out what his next move might be if we knew what he wants us to do before his deadline.'

Peyton shook his head. 'Don't try to use this situation to your advantage. I needed your help to check out whether Jesse was up there, and you gave it. I don't need you again.'

'Except you have to admit I'm right, that understanding the message will help, and you're as clueless as I. . . .' Kane trailed off when Peyton gave another one of his dismissive gestures, but this time Kane didn't mind as it made something clear. 'Again, you know.'

Peyton lowered his head for a moment and then shrugged.

'Yeah, I understood that message. The night after Pa was killed, Jesse sent me an ultimatum. I refused.'

Kane waited for an explanation, but when Peyton didn't provide one, he hazarded a guess.

'Jesse wants the same deal with you that he had with your father?'

'He does, but he's not getting it.'

'I'm pleased to hear that, but why would he want such a deal?'

'Because he likes killing, and because he's wiped out so many outlaws, the enemies he's made, mean he needs the protection of the law.'

'He must be more desperate than I'd thought and perhaps we can use that against him.'

'We're not trying nothing.' Peyton pointed at Kane until he nodded. 'We'll wait him out and force him to make the next move.'

'We will do that,' Kane said.

Kane smiled, and when Peyton registered his emphasis, muttered something to himself and headed into the house.

CHAPTER 14

'So the sheriff is sure it'll come to a head before noon tomorrow,' Driscoll said when Kane had explained the recent developments.

'He does, and I agree,' Kane said. He moved to the hotel window to look down on the main drag.

They had taken three upstairs rooms in a row, but for now were congregated in the central room.

'But you have no idea what kind of deal Jesse wants, to stop him carrying out his threat?'

Kane shook his head while still facing away from the other two men. He had been guarded in what he'd told them and hadn't mentioned his father's secret or Peyton's rejection of Jesse's ultimatum, concentrating instead on the basic facts that Jesse would act and it could involve them.

'So, we'll just do what we agreed before I went for dinner and keep our heads down until after Jesse's deadline has passed.'

He turned, expecting Driscoll to support him and Zackary to go along with this plan, as they usually did, but both men shook their heads.

'While you were away we've been talking,' Zackary said. 'We don't want to just wait for the worst to happen, even if it is for only the next night and morning.'

Kane shrugged. 'Waiting doesn't sit easy with me either, but I can't think of anything useful we can do, so unless you can come up with a plan that sounds like it might work, I reckon we should stay here.'

Kane raised an eyebrow, inviting them to outline their best idea, but both men looked aside, confirming that they didn't have one. They turned to sorting out the sleeping arrangements for the night.

They agreed that they'd all stay in this room. In three shifts, one man would sleep in the bed while the other two dozed in chairs beside the door and window.

As it turned out, it was approaching midnight before they got to sleep as they spent the rest of the evening discussing how they could find Jesse before he found them, again without coming up with a plan that felt better than staying in the hotel.

Despite their failures, when Kane awoke in the morning, having been the last one to use the bed, he ran through the information he'd learnt, and made a connection that hadn't occurred to him before. It was still dark, but he coughed, making his companions stir.

'I've had a change of heart,' he said. 'I agree with you that we shouldn't stay here, and I reckon we should go to Sheridan Pass.'

'I'm relieved to hear that,' Zackary said around a yawn. 'Jesse is probably planning to do something in Union Town, so if we can get there we'll be safe, at least for now.'

'That wasn't my thinking. I reckon we should go there because that's where Jesse will be.'

Zackary winced and Driscoll shook his head.

'You'll have to explain that to us,' Driscoll said while stretching.

'Jesse promised to act before noon today, and Virginia's husband, a US Marshal, is arriving on the noon train. I reckon that means Jesse plans to kill him, so I intend to get as far down the tracks as we can, board the train, warn him and then be in place to help him stop Jesse.'

'You could be right. Jesse has always stayed close to the rail tracks, as did Valentine and Finnegan before him, and maybe the reason was because they were waiting for the marshal.'

Kane hadn't considered that before, but even though he thought it unlikely, with both men sounding enthused about his plan, he didn't disagree. It also made him realize that whether or not Jesse had stayed close to the railroad, he might be a frequent visitor to Sheridan Pass. To have carried out his activities in secret for the last ten years, he had to have a base somewhere close to Union Town.

'If we're all agreed, we need to hurry to intercept the train,' he said.

Both men nodded, so in short order they left the hotel and collected their horses from the stable. Within ten minutes they were riding out of town.

Driscoll reckoned that they should tell Peyton about their plan, but Kane disagreed, claiming that they didn't have enough time, although in truth he reckoned that whatever the merits of Driscoll's suggestion, it would provoke another unwelcome argument.

They maintained a fast trot while staying beside the tracks, keeping a lookout for both Jesse and the train coming towards them, but the sun rose and climbed higher into the sky without incident.

Kane was familiar enough with this journey to judge how much further they had to go. When he reckoned they were an hour away from their destination, he reported this fact to the others.

His comment made them all peer ahead anxiously, as they knew that if they tried to stop the train between stations, they would probably fail. They needed to reach Sheridan Pass by mid-morning and that deadline now felt close.

They rode on for most of the next hour with still no sign of the train when something else caught their attention. A group of riders came swinging down from the north.

As the pass where they'd encountered Riley was to the north, they watched the riders with concern.

When the newcomers came close enough to discern that six men were approaching, the same number as had been in Riley's group, without comment to each other they speeded up to a gallop.

This action encouraged the riders to speed up and veer away from their previous path to head towards the town, confirming their identity and showing that they were trying to intercept them before they reached Sheridan Pass.

Kane repeatedly glanced to the side as he judged Riley's progress, and when the town first came into view, he reckoned that Riley wouldn't get there before them. He shouted this good news to the others and so, heartened, they dragged an extra burst of speed from their mounts.

Riley's men spread out as they tried to match their speed, but when Kane's group reached the first building on the edge of town, the riders were around a half-mile behind them. They still faced the problem of fending off Riley, along with their original concern that Jesse would be here, but then they had a spot of luck when the train came into view.

They headed onto the platform and dismounted in a hurry. They were the only people here and as this was a flag station, the brothers stood by the tracks and waved at the train while Kane looked in the opposite direction at Riley.

The platform was on open ground with no cover

and the nearest building was a stable around fifty yards away, although as Riley was coming from that direction, Kane dismissed this as a place to hole up.

He watched the riders and it became clear that their luck was about to run out as Riley would arrive before the train did, so he stood with his back to the others and drew his gun. When the riders came within firing range, he blasted off a couple of high shots.

This had the desired effect when the riders stopped their headlong dash towards them to take refuge behind the stable. A whistle followed by the screech of brakes sounded, so with it now clear that the train would stop, the brothers joined him, drawing their guns and taking aim at the stable.

Both men blasted off a couple of warning shots into the stable wall, after which Kane saw movement elsewhere in town. Kane feared that they had gathered Jesse's attention, but it was only people scurrying into hiding while gunshots were traded.

Then in a co-ordinated move, two of Riley's men stepped out on one side of the stable and Riley appeared on the other. The men returned fire and lead hammered into the platform around Kane's legs.

Kane took aim at the shooters, but before he could fire, Zackary and Driscoll took evasive action by leaping over the edge of the platform then lying flat. Kane followed them to lie on his chest between the tracks and the side of the platform.

The platform was high enough to shield him from being hit, but the gap wasn't wide enough for him to avoid serious injury when the train arrived in around another minute. He raised his gun on to the platform, but a slug tore splinters out of the wood to his side, forcing him to duck down again.

'Come out and die or stay there and die,' Riley shouted.

Kane shouted a defiant retort, but his words were drowned out by a prolonged blast on the whistle. He glanced over his shoulder and saw that Zackary and Driscoll were peering in alarm at the train that was now bearing down on them.

He tried again to raise his gun on to the platform and this time several shots pounded into the wood from different directions. The loud reports confirmed that Riley and his men were advancing on them to ensure they stayed down.

'We give in,' Kane shouted when the whistle stopped. 'We'll pay you double.'

'You haven't got a thousand dollars.'

Kane glanced at Zackary, who looked at the train that would arrive in a matter of moments and then nodded.

'We handed our captured outlaw over to the law for the thousand-dollar bounty on his head. We get that money tomorrow. It's yours.'

The train then gave another whistle, the sound seeming to come from above him, so Kane reckoned he couldn't wait for Riley's answer and scrambled on to the platform. Driscoll followed him while Zackary waited for another few seconds before he rolled into view.

All three men leapt to their feet to face Riley. He was standing in the centre of the platform with his men grouped around him, and to their relief, had lowered their guns.

'We're much obliged,' Riley said with a mocking smile as the train shuddered to a halt. 'It was a pleasure doing business with you.'

'We're heading back to Union Town and we'll inform Sheriff Doyle to give the bounty money to you.'

Riley nodded, still sporting a smile. Kane waited for the inevitable threat, but it wasn't forthcoming, and the reason became apparent when a loud voice spoke up behind him.

'This is US Marshal Hank Wooldridge,' the man said. 'Is there a problem here?'

'It was just a misunderstanding, now resolved,' Kane said, turning to find that the marshal was the only person to have alighted from the train.

The marshal looked past Kane at Riley. 'Is that so?'

'We've reached an agreement,' Riley said.

'Then you no longer have a reason to be here.'

Riley cast a last look at Kane and the other men before he turned away. When he was heading back towards the stable, Kane glanced around the platform and further into town, but there was still no sign of Jesse, so he relaxed and nodded to the marshal.

'We're obliged for your offer of help,' he said. 'Now we can repay you, Marshal.'

'I prefer Hank, and there's no need.'

'Except there is and when we've joined you on the train we'll explain why.'

Fifteen minutes later, the train was on its way to Union Town and Hank rubbed his chin while he considered their tale. Kane had provided enough details to make the danger clear while avoiding identifying Jesse.

'I'm pleased I've finally met Virginia's half-brother, but you've wasted a journey,' he said. 'If lawmen went into hiding every time an outlaw issued a threat, they'd never see the light of day.'

'If nothing happens, I won't judge it a wasted journey,' Kane said. 'Your wife cooked me a mighty fine green chilli stew last night and I had to do something to show my appreciation.'

The marshal smiled and then complied with their concerns by organizing them to search the three cars. When they had confirmed that Jesse wasn't already on board, the three men sat down close to Hank to enjoy the return trip to town.

On the way they encountered no trouble and the train approached Union Town ahead of time. Even though it was starting to look as if Kane's theory was wrong and they'd had a wasted journey, with the deadline less than thirty minutes away, Kane urged

Hank to let them get off the train first to see if Jesse was waiting for them.

With an amused twinkle in his eye, Hank accepted his offer. Zackary stayed with him while Kane and Driscoll alighted.

Unlike at Sheridan Pass, dozens of people were getting off and many were on the platform waiting to get on. As Kane had expected, Virginia hadn't come to meet her husband, but with that many people milling around, they couldn't be sure that Jesse wasn't lying in wait.

They returned to the train and reported the situation. With Zackary behind Hank and Kane and Driscoll ahead of him, they got off the train.

They carefully watched anyone who came close to them, but didn't see Jesse, and within five minutes the four men were riding away from the station towards Hank and Virginia's home.

With open ground around them, the further they got from town the more confident Kane grew that Jesse wouldn't appear and launch an ambush, but another fear grew: that Jesse had acted while they had been away.

That worrying possibility receded when they approached the house and Virginia emerged to greet Hank. Peyton was at her side, casting cautious glances around, although the sight of Hank's companions made him glare at them before he resumed his vigil.

'What are you doing here?' Peyton demanded

when they'd dismounted, and Hank and Virginia were hugging each other.

'I had a theory that Hank might be attacked at Sheridan Pass, but I was wrong,' Kane said.

'You being wrong isn't a . . .' Peyton trailed off from uttering what was probably going to be an unsupportive comment, when Virginia peeled away from her husband's embrace to talk to Kane.

'I'm grateful for your help,' she said.

'As am I,' Hank said before he ushered her into the house, leaving Peyton and Kane facing each other.

Peyton firmed his jaw in irritation before he headed to the corner of the corral to continue looking out for trouble. Kane asked Zackary and Driscoll to take up positions on either side of the house so that they could cover all the ways Jesse might approach.

Kane waited to see if Peyton objected, but when nothing was said, he stood by the door watching the hill to the side of the house, a place that still repre-sented the most likely place from which Jesse could be watching the house.

Peyton glanced his way and noted where he was looking.

'We have ten more minutes,' he said, his voice croaking as if it was a struggle to speak to Kane. He coughed and carried on more assuredly. 'He could be up there, but while I was on my own, I couldn't check it out.'

'Two people should be enough to scout around up there,' Kane said.

Peyton gave a terse nod, so Kane raised a hand asking him to wait for a moment and headed inside to tell the others what they planned to do. He found Virginia bustling around making coffee while Hank was sitting at the table bouncing a child on each knee, fingering a bulky envelope that he'd partly extracted from an inside pocket.

'That's a wise move,' Hank said, slotting the envelope back into his pocket. 'I can take care of things here while you and Peyton deal with this situation.'

Kane nodded and then hurried outside to join Peyton, who was explaining their intention to Zackary, along with delivering a stern warning to stay here no matter what happened. As Driscoll was looking elsewhere, having presumably received the same instructions, they mounted up and in short order, set off up the hill.

Peyton took the lead, but when he had a decent view of the top of the hill with no sign of Jesse being there, he stopped and waited for Kane to catch up with him.

'I had thought that Jesse might go after Hank, too,' he said. 'I also knew that the marshal can take care of himself.'

'Hank had the same view,' Kane said. 'But as you agree that I had a good idea, here's another one: there's a sharp incline at the side of the hill that's close enough to the house for Jesse to watch it.'

'I'd already had that thought. That's why we got a height advantage. Now we swoop down on Jesse.'

Peyton set off around the top of the hill, giving Kane only a moment to wonder whether his half-brother had just expressed approval of his actions before he galloped off after him. He caught up with Peyton as the terrain started to take away their view of the house and the incline appeared ahead.

There was no sign of Jesse, but they carried on down the hill on a diagonal route until they reached ground level. Peyton headed on for a short distance, but when the far side of the hill became visible with still no sign of Jesse, he drew back on the reins and looked around at the nearby terrain.

The plains were devoid of rocks large enough to hide a man, but the grassy and gently undulating hill provided plenty of places where their quarry could have gone to ground.

'That didn't work, but it doesn't mean he's not here somewhere,' Kane said.

Peyton didn't reply, but then the distinctive voice of Jesse Sawyer shouted out to them.

'So, the sons of Peyton Doyle have finally arrived,' he called. 'It's a pity that you're already too late.'

CHAPTER 15

Both men turned on the spot, looking for Jesse, but the slope above them and to either side appeared clear.

'Where are you, Jesse?' Peyton called.

'I'm up here waiting to shoot you at a time of my choosing,' Jesse shouted.

His boast had come from only a few dozen yards away and further up the hill, but Kane still couldn't see where Jesse was hiding.

'Why are you waiting?' Peyton said. He did as Kane had done and looked around, before dismounting then standing with his legs set wide apart facing the hill.

Kane figured Peyton's plan was to keep Jesse talking until he betrayed his position. Shooting him from on horseback would be harder than if he was standing, so Kane joined him and jumped down.

He stood ten yards to Peyton's side and turned slightly away from him so that they could watch a wider swath of the slope.

'I'm counting down the minutes until noon,' Jesse said. 'I reckon by then you'll be finished and I can kill you, unless we can strike a deal.'

'So, your threat was only that you planned to kill me at noon.' Peyton turned towards Kane, his gaze wavering around a spot thirty yards above him. 'That means I still have a few minutes.'

'My threat wasn't to kill you. I want to destroy you first. Then I'll kill you.'

'That's not the kind of talk I'd expect from a man who wants to make a deal with me.'

Peyton was now looking at a point up the hill. When Kane narrowed his eyes, he saw a dip in the ground that might provide enough cover to hide Jesse.

Peyton waited for a reply, but long moments passed in silence, perhaps showing that Jesse reckoned he had offered so many taunts he might have divulged his location. Peyton smiled and caught Kane's eye before gesturing up the hill while edging his hand towards his holster.

Getting his meaning, Kane walked to the base of the slope while placing a hand on his holster. When this action didn't invite retaliation, he accepted that even if Jesse was keeping out of their sight, that worked both ways and he probably didn't have a clear view of what they were doing.

He drew his gun, as did Peyton, and then set off up the slope towards the side of the area where they suspected Jesse was hiding. He covered half the distance and when the dip in the ground became more clearly visible, he could see that it was around twenty feet long.

Kane's best guess was that Jesse had spoken from the end of the dip that was nearest to him, but by now, could have moved to another part of the hollow and still be able to surprise them. He stopped and gestured at Peyton then at the hill, trying to indicate the extent of the area where Jesse could be holed up, and then pointed at his lips.

'I'm still waiting to hear your latest offer for this deal,' Peyton called, taking Kane's hint that he should try to force Jesse to talk. He waited, but when Jesse didn't reply, he continued. 'If you don't want to discuss that, tell me how you plan to destroy me at noon.'

Peyton waited again, but still Jesse didn't reply. He looked at Kane and then at the sun conveying that it must be almost noon and Jesse was likely to act before much longer.

Kane nodded and then levelled his gun on the dip before setting off slowly up the slope. He'd taken another two steps when in a sudden movement, Jesse darted up.

He appeared at the furthest extent of the hollow away from Kane and already had his gun thrust out. With a quick motion, Jesse blasted lead at Peyton, who cried out in pain and dropped his gun.

As Peyton's hand rose up to clutch his wounded upper arm, Kane swung his gun round towards Jesse, but before he could even aim at him, Jesse ducked from view. At the bottom of the hill, Peyton dropped to his knees and reached for the gun with his left hand, but a shot rang out, winging it away from him.

This time Kane hadn't even caught a glimpse of Jesse and worse, Peyton then keeled over to lie on his side. Kane snarled in anger and hurried up the slope.

In a matter of moments, he covered most of the ten paces to put him level with the dip. The full extent of the area was coming into view when Jesse bobbed up again.

He was closer to Kane than the previous time he'd appeared, and had his gun aimed at him. Seeing that he had no choice, Kane lowered his weapon.

'I'd guess this means Peyton won't be making a deal,' Jesse said with a smirk.

'Which sure is bad news for you,' Kane said. 'Without the protection of the law, all those people you've annoyed over the years will be coming for you.'

'Do you really think that concerns someone like me?' Jesse snapped, his clipped tones confirming that Kane's taunt had been a valid one.

'I do, because why else are you giving Peyton a chance to side with you?'

147

Jesse shook his head. 'It's noon now. That chance has gone.'

'So that means it's time for you to destroy him, I guess,' Kane said, both fishing for information and playing for time.

'It is, but you don't have to be alive to see it happen.'

Jesse narrowed his eyes with a hint that he was about to fire, but at the same moment something moved behind Jesse, the distraction making Kane glance that way. Jesse chuckled and shook his head at what he thought was Kane's feeble attempt to distract him.

Jesse firmed his gun hand, but a gunshot peeled out, making Jesse twitch and drop to his knees. A moment later, Jesse twisted sideways to lie flat, out of Kane's sight.

His motion had been so quick Kane didn't reckon he had fallen because he'd been wounded. He looked to the side and saw Zackary hunkered down further up the hill with his gun aimed at Jesse's position.

Kane nodded to him in gratitude for his failure to follow Peyton's orders and then glanced at Peyton, who was now on his feet and moving towards his gun. He was bent over and his progress was slow and pained, so even though Kane judged that he would be fine if he got him to help soon, he doubted that Peyton would be able to assist him and Zackary take on Jesse.

With his gun trained on the last place he'd seen Jesse, Kane moved up the slope while Zackary set off walking down the hill. Zackary covered the ground quickly, although Kane walked sideways, slowly crossing his legs over each other as he ensured his gun never wavered in its aim.

More of the dip appeared until Kane could see along its entire length, but as he'd yet to see Jesse, he stopped and waited for Zackary to get closer. Jesse must have been aware that the situation was turning against him, and he leapt up out of the hollow and threw himself down the slope sideways.

His unexpected action surprised Kane so much he didn't fire, but once over his shock, he jerked his gun to the side and tried to follow Jesse's progress. Jesse rolled twice before thrusting out an arm, coming to a halt with his upper body slightly raised and his gun already aimed at Kane.

Kane fired at Jesse while still moving his gun. The motion made his shot slice into the ground several feet away from his target and gave Jesse enough time to return fire, but Jesse's gun arm wavered before it homed in on Kane.

This unexpected slowness drew Kane's attention to the patch of blood on Jesse's side, showing that Zackary had hit him with his earlier gunshot, after all. Heartened, Kane took the time to aim more carefully before he fired.

His shot pounded into the part of Jesse's upper chest that he could see, but Jesse still twitched his

149

trigger-finger, the lead whistling by Kane's ear. Then Jesse flopped down.

A shot from Zackary rang out, but Jesse began rolling down the slope and the slug furrowed into the ground. He went tumbling over and over while making no attempt to still his progress and crashed down at the base of the slope.

Jesse rolled on twice more. By now, Peyton had gathered up his gun, which he trained on Jesse who shuddered to a halt.

'You were right, Jesse,' Peyton said through gritted teeth. 'I won't be making a deal with you.'

Jesse didn't respond, but with Peyton sporting a pained expression that showed he was struggling to stay in control, Kane hurried down the slope to check on Jesse. Zackary also hurried on and the two men reached the bottom of the hill at the same time. Zackary trained his gun on Jesse, his action making Peyton sigh with relief and drop to his knees before sitting. Kane watched him until Peyton indicated that he was fine, and moved on to stand in front of Jesse.

Jesse was lying on his back and his chest was still moving, his breath wheezing in and out of his mouth. He didn't look at Kane, so Kane moved forward so that his shadow covered Jesse's face.

Jesse's eyes rolled to the side to consider Kane and then returned to looking straight up.

'I guess you won't be doing any destroying now,' Kane said.

'You're too late,' Jesse wheezed, his breath so shallow Kane could barely hear the words. 'I've already destroyed you all.'

Jesse forced a thin smile. Then his mouth dropped open and his head rocked to the side.

Kane knelt and shook him, but Jesse didn't speak again.

CHAPTER 16

Kane stood up and considered Jesse's still form. When he accepted that the man was dead, he studied Peyton, who was sitting hunched over, clutching his bloodied arm, and then turned to Zackary.

'Stay with Peyton and help him get back to the house,' he said.

When Zackary nodded, Kane ran off along the base of the hill. He didn't know what Jesse's final words had meant, but he felt sure they had to involve Virginia or her husband.

The most likely possibility was that Jesse had an accomplice that nobody knew about, who had waited until Jesse lured them away before launching an attack, but when the house came into sight, Driscoll was still standing guard outside. Driscoll peered at him anxiously, although Kane didn't see any sign that this was as a result of something unexpected having taken place.

Kane ran on and only paused to catch his breath when he was close enough to shout to Driscoll.

'Jesse's dead, but you still need to look out for trouble,' he called between gasps for breath.

Driscoll relayed this information to the house, while not identifying Jesse, then returned to peering around. Kane carried on until he reached the corral fence where he held on to a post while taking deep breaths. Then, with Driscoll staying outside, he headed inside.

Hank was standing guard beside the window in the main room while Virginia was sitting with her children at the back of the room.

'So, Valentine's associate is dead, but you fear another one is out there?' Hank said.

'I reckon something might still happen, but I don't know what,' Kane said and then faced Virginia. 'Peyton has been wounded, but he's fine. He'll arrive shortly with Zackary and he'll need patching up.'

'I'll deal with that,' Virginia said with a worried gulp.

While she busied herself with locating bandages, Kane joined Hank by the window. For the next few minutes they kept a silent vigil, but saw nothing until Zackary and Peyton came trudging into view.

Driscoll moved away from the house to help them, making Hank and Kane stand up straight as this might be the moment when trouble arrived, but Driscoll joined Zackary without incident. Then they took an arm apiece to escort Peyton to the house.

Virginia hurried to the door and opened it. Then she fussed over Peyton while he was taken to the table and made to sit down.

'Everything fine?' he asked, looking at Kane.

'It is, but then again it's hard to confirm that this is over now,' Kane said.

His declaration made the brothers head back outside and Peyton presented his arm to Virginia so that she could help him out of his jacket. As she set about assessing the damage, Hank cast another look out of the window and then headed to the other end of the table.

'You're right, but noon has come and gone,' he declared. 'For the next few days we'll continue to be cautious, but for now we should relax and return to our normal business.'

Then, emphasizing his point, he withdrew the letter he'd been fingering earlier, from his inside pocket. While watching Virginia get to work cutting open Peyton's bloodied shirt sleeve, he tapped the letter against his other hand, drawing Kane's attention to it.

A worrying thought came to Kane.

'What's in the letter?' he asked lightly.

'I don't know,' Hank said. 'I was given it on the train with instructions to read it when I reached Union Town. It could be nothing, but I assume that it's business for a US Marshal's eyes only.'

Hank maintained a soft tone as he gave his mild rebuke, but it made Kane gulp while Peyton cast a concerned look at the letter.

'It could be a warning about the next trouble we'll face,' Kane said, coming over to the table. 'We may need to act quickly.'

Hank shrugged while gesturing with the letter. When he didn't show any sign that he would hand it over without reading it first, Kane wondered whether he should let the situation play itself out, but didn't reckon Virginia deserved to learn the truth this way.

He stepped forward and snatched the letter from Hank's hand.

Hank grunted in anger. 'You may be family, but that doesn't give you the right to interfere in my duties.'

Hank held out a hand, but Kane backed away from the table.

'Maybe it doesn't, but I heard the final words that Valentine's associate uttered and I know more about this situation than you do.'

Hank didn't reply as he thrust out his hand more forcefully.

'Give it back, Kane,' Virginia said, this unexpected altercation making her furrow her brow. 'We're all under stress and there's no need to make things worse.'

Kane glanced at Peyton, who returned a concerned look, so he shook his head and sliced open the letter. He perused the folded paper inside and although he didn't see Jesse Sawyer's name written down, he saw Sheriff Cornelius Doyle's name numerous times along with several worrying revelations.

With his fears confirmed that Jesse had written this letter, Kane could only conclude that it detailed the criminal activities that the former sheriff had turned a blind eye to, over the last ten years. These were revelations that a principled lawman like Hank couldn't ignore, so he turned to the door.

'I have a hunch about what this means, so I'll back it and return presently.'

'You won't,' Hank snapped as he leapt to his feet so quickly he upturned his chair. 'I'm a fine judge of character and I can tell you just lied. You're not leaving until I know what you're hiding from me.'

Kane winced, but still tucked the envelope in his jacket pocket and walked away with Hank following behind. He'd reached the door and was moving to open it when Hank grabbed his shoulder.

Kane spun round to face him while bunching a fist, then used the speed of his pivot to crunch a blow into Hank's chin; it cracked his head back before he toppled over to land on his back.

'Don't stand in my way,' Kane said. 'I'm acting for the benefit of everyone in this family.'

Hank glared at him while rubbing his chin, but made no move to get back up other than to point a warning finger at him.

'Do what you have to do, but afterwards, I will see what's in that letter,' he declared. 'Then I'll charge you for that punch. Being family doesn't excuse criminal behaviour.'

'And that's the problem,' Kane said quietly as he prised the door open with his heel while still facing Hank.

He backed away through the opening as Virginia hurried across the room to kneel beside Hank, and when the marshal signified that he would be fine, she looked at Kane with her eyes blazing.

'I won't ever invite you for dinner again,' she said. 'You're no longer welcome here.'

She got up and slammed the door in his face. Kane lowered his head and sighed. Then he turned to Zackary and Driscoll.

'It's time to go,' he said.

'It does seem quiet out here, but what just happened in there?' Driscoll said.

'My brother still hates me, my sister now hates me and my brother-in-law wants to arrest me.' Kane smiled. 'Aside from that, everything's fine.'

Driscoll grinned. 'I guess we don't need to have that explained just yet, but it sounds as if we ought to leave quickly.'

The three men headed to their horses and when they were mounted, moved to leave the corral, but before they could ride away, Peyton came out of the house. He closed the door behind him and with a hand clutched to his loosely-bandaged upper arm, came over to stand in front of Kane's horse.

'I'm grateful for what you just did,' he said. 'I'll talk Hank out of arresting you for that punch, but I assume that letter details our father's activities?'

Kane nodded. 'I only had time for a brief glance at it, but I reckon it listed the men he'd had killed while not mentioning that Jesse was the killer.'

'Hank is a good man and despite the harm it'd do, he couldn't have ignored an allegation as serious as that. He'd have carried out a full investigation and nothing good would have come of it.'

'That much is certain,' Kane said with a rueful sigh. 'That's why I'm keeping the letter until I can work out what's the least worst way to deal with making sure the truth comes out.'

Kane braced himself for another outburst, but Peyton only nodded.

'I'll be the one who works that out. This has never been about ensuring the truth remains buried. It'll come out one day, but not while our father is still fresh in the ground, and not because of Jesse Sawyer's act of revenge.'

Kane breathed a sigh of relief. 'Then I'll let you decide how to do it, but I'm leaving town now, so you'll have to find a plausible excuse to explain what's in the letter to keep Hank content until that day comes.'

'There are some matters that a sheriff doesn't have to explain fully, so I already have a lie in mind. For it to work, I need you to leave town on an unspecified mission.'

'I can do that for you. In return, that varmint, Riley Payne, will soon pester you for our bounty money.' Kane glanced at Zackary and Driscoll, who both nodded. 'Make sure he gets it, and then there'll be no reason why you should ever see me again.'

'There isn't, but you didn't let me finish explaining my plan.' Peyton smiled. 'For it to work, you'll need to come back in a few months and apologize to Hank, and probably take a punch to the jaw without complaint.'

Kane considered Peyton, noting that this had been the first time he had smiled at him.

'Do you reckon that Virginia will have forgiven me by then?'

'She'll still be annoyed with you, but I reckon in the end she'll accept what happened.'

'Even when she learns that I am, in fact, the man who shot Jesse Sawyer?'

'Even then, as that'll mean you have something in common with our father.' Peyton turned to head to the house, but then stopped and turned back. 'Welcome to the family. We have some difficult times ahead.'

With that, he moved on to the house.

Kane watched him until he'd gone inside and closed the door. Then he looked at the window, but the people inside weren't visible, so he turned away.

Zackary and Driscoll both smiled at him and the

three men rode away at a slow trot. They headed towards the rail tracks, but on a route that would take them in the opposite direction to Green Valley and the other towns that they had all visited recently.

A few miles on, Kane slowed down to let the brothers take the lead. He knew that the house would no longer be visible, but that didn't stop him from looking over his shoulder.

He stayed gazing back for a short while. Then he smiled and hurried on to ride alongside the others.